SEIZED BY OBSCURITY

Evergreen Series I

BY

JOANN HERLEY

ISBN-10: 0692401040
ISBN-13: 978-0692401040

ACKNOWLEDGEMENTS

Cover Illustration by: © Konstantin Yuganov | Dreamstime.com

DEDICATION

To my husband, Gene, for his endless love and encouragement.

To my granddaughters, Sadie Magnolia and Scarlett Blue,
for sharing the love of fantasy and vampires with me.
I think of you every day.

SPECIAL THANKS

To Pam Maier for taking the time to read my first manuscript. Your enthusiasm kept me motivated to continue the journey of Lara and Thomas. Your desire to see the wicked defeated, kept my imagination fired up!

History of the Island of Alltree

Long ago, explorers in strong ships discovered its lush forests, fertile earth and crystal clear rivers. Hearing of the beauty of the land, Lady Lara's grandfather, Lord Evergreen, boarded a ship and sailed to the Island of Alltree to see the land for himself. Captured by its beauty, he returned home to tell every one of the faraway island and his plans to build Evergreen Castle. Returning to Alltree with skilled craftsmen, he proceeded to build a castle on the west side of the island that overlooked the sea. After a decade, his castle was finally complete, and he proudly brought his family to their new home.

One by one Lord Cumberland, Lord Fallon, Lord Draglaw, and Lord Heinrich made the journey to Alltree and began building castles of their own. They were all peace loving men, and the five lords pledged to refrain from war and live in peace.

It wasn't long before immortals heard rumors of the island. They began to sneak aboard the ships heading to Alltree. With their arrival, they changed everything.

Prologue

Thomas sat alone in his bed chamber at the Evergreen Castle. He let his mind travel back to the night she had found him. It was shortly after he had been turned that she had brought him safely through the struggle and anguish of blood and killing. Allowing his mind to continue to wander, he painfully remembered how it all began.

His family had been tortured and killed by a band of blood thirsty thieves. While he had been working the fields of a neighbor, he saw the plume of black smoke rising in the sky. Running home, he found the remains of the cottage, he had helped his father build, consumed in flames. His family was dead, scattered on the ground among the burning embers. Falling to his knees, grief ripped at his chest, and he swore revenge for their horrible murder.

Tenderly, he wrapped his parents and two sisters in bed linens left scattered among the bushes from the morning's wash. He carefully dug four graves within the small family cemetery behind the cottage. While weeping, he buried them alongside the wooden markers of his grandparents.

His brother, Tate, was all that was left of the family. Tate had left, many years ago, to work the big ships that carried goods to faraway places. With every ship that brought goods back to Echo Bluff, their mother would watch the dirt road. She would stand at the window waiting for his return. She never gave up hope of seeing him again. Now, Thomas hoped to see his brother. He needed Tate, now more than ever.

Exhausted from the ordeal, Thomas gathered the few remaining bed linens from the bushes. Making a bed for the night under the stars, Thomas thought of his family. Closing his eyes, he prayed for their souls and the strength to avenge their murders. Sleep came quickly, but his dreams turned to nightmares filled with visions of fire, smoke, screaming and death. The nightmares continued for weeks. To deaden the pain, he spent many days and nights in the local tavern drinking, gambling and playing with women.

One night after his coin was finally gone, he staggered out the tavern door and down the dirt road leading back toward the remains of the only home he had ever known. He had no thoughts for his safety or of his death. Many times, he had wished death would take pity on him and just end it all. Stumbling through the dense cover of darkness, he could see something off in the distance. A tall sliver of a man with long silver hair and glowing red eyes stepped from the thick fog.

The ale must be playing tricks upon my mind, he thought, as he rubbed his eyes to see more clearly.

As he got closer to the stranger, he saw what he thought were long sharp fangs extending from the man's mouth. Without seeing the man move, he suddenly felt a sharp piercing pain as his vision began to blur into darkness.

"Do you have need of your life young man?" asked the stranger. Licking the blood from his lips with his tongue, he looked down upon the face of his victim. Hearing no response, the stranger asked again but louder, "Do you want to live beyond this dark night?"

Thomas found it difficult to move, but he wanted to live. He succeeded in only giving the stranger a slight nod. Seeing the affirming response of his victim's head within his hands, the stranger pierced deep into his victim's neck with his fangs. Draining the last of life's blood from his body, the stranger felt the beat of his heart fade to silence. The stranger quickly pulled away and tore his own wrist with his fangs. Forcing the blood from his wrist into his victim's mouth, Thomas fought to pull away from his grasp. As the blood ran across his tongue, the taste and scent of the alluring liquid caused him to latch onto the open wound. Thomas drank, until he was no longer conscious.

When Thomas woke, the stranger was gone. His throat was burning like someone had forced a flaming torch into his mouth. Screaming in pain, he stumbled as he tried to stand. Trying once more, he somehow made it to his feet. He felt something wet running down his neck and over his chest. Rubbing his hand against his neck, he pulled his hand away to see blood on his palm. Panicking, he ran wildly into the forest afraid the attacker would return. Tripping over large roots covered in moss, his hands and knees sank into the soggy earth. Trying to regain his footing, he felt the stings from the sharp thorns of branches that scraped against his legs. Hearing the sound of water, he hurried toward the nearby stream. Finally reaching the rushing water, he fell face first into the crisp cool water and let it cover his body. He began swallowing as much water as he could to stop the burning, but no amount of water would stop the pain. He tore at his tunic and gripped at his throat. Screaming in anguish, he tried to stand and slipped on the damp moss along the stream's edge. Letting his body collapse to the ground, he closed his eyes trying to endure the pain and rested his face against the cool moss until the darkness took him from the pain.

From that point until she found him, he killed anyone or anything for blood. The madness had found him and easily seized his mind and body. He reveled in the thrill of the hunt, and the taste of the sweet red liquid was his reward.

Chapter 1

L ate one evening while walking through the village, Lara heard the merriment of laughter and music coming from inside the tavern. She made her way through the door and looked about for an empty table. Finding a small table in the far corner away from the men wildly playing cards, she took a seat. She looked about the tavern feeling a strange and unexpected pulling of her mind. The sensation grew stronger as she searched the dim room for the cause. Spotting a man walk through the tavern door and sit down at an empty bench, she realized he was the source of the sensation.

She watched him slam his hand upon the small wooden table. He was clearly out of control and barely hid the fact that he was not human. She was sure he was a vampire and held deep within the control of madness. His eyes were rimmed in deep red and showed the desperate need for blood. He was a tall man of muscular build with dark brown hair that fell in waves beyond his shoulders. His clothes were torn and dirty making it clear he hadn't bathed recently. The stubble upon his face was lightly frosted with gray, a sure sign he was much older at his turning. As he looked about the tavern, the bit of silvergray within the red rim of his eyes caught Lara's attention. There was a sadness within his eyes and an even sadder story hidden within his mind.

Men scattered within the tavern wanting to keep their distance from him, feeling trouble would be their end. He yelled for ale and grabbed the arm of a woman as she passed by his table to make his request clear. He was rough and had a mouth that would make the local priest faint.

There was something about this vampire that she could not figure out. Determined to know why, she sat several nights within the tavern watching him come and go. Each night as he entered the tavern, the strange sensation was present. When he left the tavern, the sensation slowly faded away.

This one night after many of the locals had left full of ale and staggering for home, Thomas sat at a rickety table with a buxom young red head woman hanging all over him. After a few ales were gulped, he wiped his mouth with his soiled sleeve. Whispering in her ear, the young woman nodded as she grinned seeing the coin within the palm of his dirty hand. They stood, and he held her tightly around the waist. Her feet barely touched the floor while bursting through the side door to the alley. Knowing what was about to happen, Lara followed the pair into the darkness of the muddy alley.

"Stop," shouted Lara, as she was instantly standing between Thomas and the young woman. She grabbed the woman by the arm and pushed her aside. "Run! You are in great danger here." Seeing the woman's confused stare, Lara pulled her gift of compulsion and looked into the woman's eyes as she sternly stated, "Leave now. Get away from this place."

The young woman quickly backed away tripping on the hem of her skirt and losing a shoe in the mud. Snatching it quickly, she stood and lifted the hem of her skirt as she ran from the alley without looking back.

"Get out of my way woman," shouted Thomas, as he raised his arm and tried to backhand Lara across the face.

Lara effortlessly stopped his hand with her arm and pushed him back making him stumble within the thick mud. Angered, Thomas let his fangs descend and ran at Lara, ready to end her life. Just as he raised his hand to reach for her, his eyes locked upon her crystal blue eyes. His breath caught halting his arm in midair, and his brows lowered in puzzlement over his eyes. Confused, he stared at the small woman before him.

"What are you? Witch?" Thomas asked, as he fell to one knee feeling weakened by her gaze. "What spell have you cast upon me?"

"I am like you, a vampire," she softly spoke. Bending toward him, she touched the side of his face with the back of her hand. "My name is Lara, and if you would allow me, I would like to help you."

"Like me? How can this be? I am a man consumed with the taste of blood and killing," he said, as he lowered his head and closed his eyes. Growling, he clenched his fists as he inhaled her sweet scent. "My desire for the taste of blood never stops. It is all that I desire." Looking back into her eyes, he let his tongue flick from the corner of his mouth as he thought of tasting her. Trying to control his thoughts, he released a sudden nervous laugh. "I have become quite good at persuading unsuspecting ladies into bed or the alleys outside the taverns in return for a few coins. My mouth enjoys the taste of their body and their sweet blood." Feeling a slight sense of shame, he lowered his head again. "I have killed men simply because they were in my way or for the need of their coins." Afraid that she would leave him after hearing his confession, he raised his head to search her blue eyes. Kindness gazed back at him. "You appear to be an angel filled with nothing but goodness. Only an angel could make me feel this warmth within my dead chest." Trying to show her what he meant, Thomas placed his hands against his chest and felt a slight warmth beneath his palms.

"Please, let me help you," Lara asked, as she bent down reaching for his hands. "Let me help you."

Thomas pulled away from her touch. He felt the madness and feared it would make him harm her. Her scent was more than he could stand, and he wanted to taste her blood swirl upon his tongue. Wanting to leave, he stood and backed away to keep her safe. Seeing her take a step toward him, he willed himself to be strong. He felt his body stiffen, and he clenched his fists to remain perfectly still.

"I can show you how to control this dreadful madness. I can assure you that it will not be easy to let go of it, but once you have done so, you will know great relief. You will know that it was worth it." Looking into his eyes, she could see the conflict that raged within him. "Please trust me. I promise that I will help you. If my offer pleases you, give me your name and take my hand so that you may come with me," offered Lara, as she offered her small hand to him.

Feeling his need for her, he stepped forward. The scent of her blood was intoxicating. As he started to grab her arm, he looked into her eyes and stood frozen in place. He could not harm her and needed her help. His mind told him that he needed her. Hesitating, he looked down at her small fragile hand and extended his own as he spoke, "My name is Thomas."

Lara took hold of his large callused hand and whispered a few short words into the wind. Instantly they vanished.

* * *

Lara paced just outside the door of the Holding Room and was anxious for Thomas to wake and start his recovery. She had made it her life's work to help humans that had been turned and provide new vampires with shelter within her castle. She was unmated and the adored Mistress of Evergreen Castle. Even though she was a small woman, she had perfected her gifted powers and achieved high praise from the commander of her army for her skill with a sword and dagger. She was strong willed, as well as, a compassionate vampire that ruled Evergreen Castle with one rule: Never drink human blood.

Thomas was secured far below the castle's main quarters. This room was constructed especially for humans that had been turned by vampires and needed the madness driven from their body. The ceiling was high with an iron candle chandelier hanging from the center. A small hearth sheltered burning logs to take the dampness from the room. The thick stone walls and floor prevented the screams from being heard throughout the castle. The shackles for his wrists were spelled to prevent an escape, but they still allowed movement around the room to the chair, table and bed provided for some comfort.

Since flashing from outside the tavern to the Evergreen Castle, Thomas had fallen unconscious. It had been five days since flashing, and the effects of the sudden journey found him still sleeping. She had made sure that he was bathed and dressed in clean clothes. Driving the madness from Thomas would not be easy. It was never easy to rid the madness that seized a vampire's mind, but Lara knew it was worth the struggle. Thomas would be no different than the others. However, Lara felt a connection to this vampire and needed to find out why.

Sensing that Thomas was starting to wake, she entered the room and stood at a distance watching him slowly open his eyes. As he realized that he was restrained, anger swelled within him, and he struggled to release his arms from the chains that held him. The more he struggled the angrier he became. His fangs fully descended, and his eyes burned a bright red as he flung his arms trying to loosen the cuffs about his wrists.

"What have you done to me, woman? Why am I held here in these chains?" Thomas snarled. He wildly looked about the room for some way to escape. Bringing his focus back to the woman that stood before him, he watched her take a step toward him. Taking a step toward her, he stopped when he felt the pull on his wrists.

"It is for your protection and the protection of others that I have brought you here," Lara softly replied, as she stepped closer to Thomas. "Do you not remember me finding you in the muddy alley? You were about to feed upon a young woman, and I stopped you."

Thomas continued to struggle against the chains hoping they would pull from the stone wall and allow him to escape from his prison. "Yes, I remember having my meal torn from me, and I remember you said something of helping me. Is this how you intend on helping me? You have me chained to a wall in a cell," he shouted, as he lunged at Lara. He felt the desire for a taste of her blood fill his mind. Nostrils flaring, he inhaled the sweet scent of her blood.

"Try to calm yourself," Lara replied. "This is just the beginning stage, and I must secure you to help stifle the madness. Sadly, this will take many nights. I will do my best to help you through this and keep you from harming yourself." Taking a few steps closer to Thomas, she saw the cuffs were beginning to rub the skin from his wrists.

"I need to feed! Woman, my throat is burning! I must feed to make the pain go away!" Thomas clenched his throat with his hands and fell to the floor. He brought his knees to his chest as he gripped his throat.

Lara knew it had been some time since he had fed. It was time to start weaning him off the desire for human blood. She signaled for Charlotte to bring the pitcher of animal blood. As Charlotte entered the Holding Room, Thomas looked up. His deep red eyes followed her as she moved across the room. His nostrils flared as he took in the scent of the young woman and felt his mouth water in anticipation of the taste of her sweet blood.

"You have brought me a fine young blood meal," smirked Thomas, as he stood and moved as close as he could to the young woman. His mouth continued to water as he ran his tongue against the points of his fangs.

"Charlotte is not your blood meal!" Lara sternly stated. "No humans here at this castle are to be used as blood meals. Your blood meal will be animal blood today and all days hereafter." Lara accepted the pitcher from Charlotte and nodded toward the chamber door. "Leave, my dear, and lock the door behind you."

She stepped to the small table. Picking up the pewter cup, Thomas watched as she poured the blood filling it half way to the rim. Stepping toward Thomas, she started to raise the cup toward him just as Thomas knocked it from her hand and screamed, "Animal blood is foul smelling and tastes of bitterness! I will not drink the blood of dead animals. I want to drink the rich sweetness of human blood. I want to drink your blood."

Lara retrieved the cup and set it upon the table. She pulled the chair beside the hearth toward the table and sat down gracefully frowning at Thomas. He watched her every move and felt the need to sink his fangs into her neck, to drain her blood, and remove her head from her body for keeping him a prisoner.

"My head will stay firmly on my shoulders, and you will do better to think of something else," Lara responded, as she glared at Thomas forcing him to look directly into her eyes.

Thomas looked stunned, realizing that she could read his thoughts. As he looked into her eyes, he felt a calmness come over him. He could see a light about her that shown of silver and blue hues. It made her look heavenly.

"What is this light that shines about you?" Thomas asked, as he leaned against the stone wall of the chamber. "You said that you are a vampire, but you have the glow of an angel from heaven. Do you hide your wings from me? If so, turn so that I may see your wings." Seeing her shake her head, he felt confused. "Is this my mind playing tricks on me?"

"I am not playing tricks with your sight or your mind, and I am not an angel. I am a vampire, like you. This light is my protection spell given to me by a witch. She lives here within this castle and is faithful to me and the people that live here. She has helped me save many vampires like yourself and will assist me in helping you." Lara stood again and walked to the table where the pitcher of animal blood rested. She poured another cup of blood and walked toward Thomas. "We will try again to quench your thirst with the taste of animal blood," Lara said, as she held the cup out toward Thomas.

This time he took it and sniffed the cup before taking a gulp of the deep red liquid. He gagged for her benefit but finished the remaining blood knowing it was this or nothing. Throwing the cup to the floor, Thomas grunted and wiped his mouth with the back of his hand. He stepped back and returned to the wall and slid down until he sat upon the stone floor. Annoyed with his display, Lara shook her head and walked across the room to the door.

"I will leave the pitcher for you, if you find you require more. Try to rest, I will return later this evening to see how you are doing," Lara spoke, as she opened the heavy door. Looking over her shoulder, she saw him lower his eyes to the floor before she closed the door leaving Thomas alone.

Thomas stood and quickly moved to the table where the pitcher remained. He picked up the pitcher bringing it to his mouth and drank until the pitcher was empty. It was nasty tasting, but it relieved the burn in his throat and left him feeling somewhat satisfied. Spotting the bed, he made his way over to it and sat down on the feather mattress. Removing his boots and untying his vest from the sides, he pulled the vest over his head. Throwing it on the floor beside his boots, he laid back upon the bed.

He closed his eyes and thought of his family for the first time since he was turned. He would never hear their stories or laughter ever again. He longed for his sisters to dance with him in the evening and sing old songs with wonderful harmonious lyrics. He missed the way his mother filled the air with aromas of rabbit stew and freshly baked bread. He would never hear his father chopping wood, or smell the strong tobacco from his pipe. His brother had been gone for many years working on the big ships, and his memories of Tate were of a tall skinny boy chasing rabbits for his mother. These memories had been lost since the turning, and it seemed odd that they had come back to him now. It was nice to have them back, and it made him smile for a moment as he was finally able to relax. Slipping slowly into sleep, he dreamt of his family and of Lara.

* * *

As Lara entered the chamber, he woke from his sleep and sat up quickly looking about the room. Rubbing his hands over his face and through his hair, he looked up to find Lara standing before him.

"I find you resting? Do you wish me to leave and come back later?" she asked and turned back toward the door.

"No, you may stay," Thomas replied, continuing to rub his hands through his hair and then dropping his hands to let them rest upon his thighs. Looking at the floor, he waited for her to speak.

Lara moved the chair closer to the bed and sat down facing him. Straightening the folds of her skirt, she placed her hands in her lap. She raised her head, and her eyes took in the strong bulk of his chest and shoulders. His large callused hands rested upon his thick thighs, and she thought, for only a moment, of what it might be like to have his strong arms wrapped around her. She blinked her eyes to regain her purpose and softly asked, "Did you sleep well?"

"I dreamt of my home and my family," he replied trying not to let her know the things he had dreamt about her. "They are no longer living, and I miss them."

"Can you tell me of your family? If it would be too hurtful, I would understand your denial," she asked. Seeing the sadness in his eyes, she knew that he missed them and must have loved them dearly.

Thomas told Lara of his brother that went away to work the ships. He hoped one day he would return but was afraid of how he would react when he found out he was a vampire. He sobbed as he spoke of his sisters and parents and finding them slaughtered. His temper flared as revenge for their deaths consumed his body, and he shook his hands trying to release the shackles.

"I should be hunting down the murderers, but instead, I am held here in this room speaking to you of dreams and memories," yelled Thomas, as he stood and punched at the stone walls. Seeing blood on his knuckles and feeling no relief, he leaned against the stone wall and tried to still his thoughts.

"There will be time enough to find the murderers of your family. But first, we must get you strong and free of human blood. I can see that your mind has already started to rebuild and has started to release some of the madness," she replied, as she heard footsteps coming toward the chamber door.

There was a light knock at the door, and Charlotte entered the chamber carrying another pitcher. Thomas sniffed the air and smiled at the young woman. He could sense that she was frightened as he watched her look for reassurance from Lara. She placed the pitcher on the table and turned to leave the room.

"Young woman? Come and sit with me as I drink the meal that you so kindly brought me this evening," chuckled Thomas.

Charlotte looked over her shoulder and blushed as she left the room. Her only response was the sound of the lock being snapped into place. Thomas caught Lara's raised eyebrow, as he looked at her to measure her reaction.

Is she angry at my words or have I made her a little jealous?

Lara responded only with a huff after hearing his thoughts.

"May I ask you a question?" Thomas asked, as he made his way back to the bed and sat down. He carefully watched her face for an expression of anger.

Lara nodded as she smiled back at him, "Of course."

"Have you always been a vampire or were you turned?" he nervously asked, as he waited for her response.

Lara stood and looked about the Holding Room before she spoke, as if sending her mind back to another time. She rarely thought about her turning, and when she did, it brought memories of her parents and friends that died long ago.

"It was over two hundred years ago that I was turned. I lived here, in the castle with my parents, Lord and Lady Evergreen, and my younger sister, Magna. For my eighteenth birthday, my parents gave me a beautiful sable stallion with white markings about his ankles. I named him Major and spent every day riding and caring for him. One evening, a stranger wandered into the stable and found me carrying fresh water to Major's stall. I dropped the wooden pails and turned to run back to the castle. He quickly caught me and pulled me into an empty stall. I saw his red eyes, and his silver hair hung over my face.

He wrapped his arms around my body, and I felt a horrible stinging pain in my neck. The next thing I knew, my father was picking me up in his arms and carrying me back to my room. My parents had heard the stories of vampires and seeing the marks upon my neck, now knew that they were true. I was kept in this room, where you are now, as my parents cared for me and taught me to drink animal blood. With their help, I grew stronger and could walk within the castle without them worrying that I would harm someone. They kept me from becoming a monster. I lived with them until their death. It was then, I became Mistress of Evergreen. I have cared for others as I care for you, now. I do this to honor my parents, for the love they showed me when they could have easily had me slain," she closed her eyes as she finished telling her story letting visions of her parents pass through her mind.

"Did you never take a husband or lover?" Thomas asked, as he watched her face to see if he had offended her over such a personal question.

Lara sighed and took a moment to gather her thoughts before she spoke. "My parents had arranged a marriage for me at my birth. His name was Charles, and he lived at the Cumberland Castle many days journey from Evergreen Castle. We were married when I reached the age of sixteen, and I moved from Evergreen Castle to live with him. He was five years older than myself, quiet and kind. He loved to ride and hunt with his brothers. One day, the hunting party was caught in a sudden storm, far beyond the waterfalls of Witches Weep before they could return home. Charles spent the night in the storm without shelter and returned home unconscious, with a fever. He died three days later. After his death, my parents brought me back to Evergreen Castle, where I have lived to this day. I was married for only fifty-two days."

Thomas could see the sadness in her eyes and was sorry that he had asked such a personal question.

* * *

Every morning and every evening, Lara came to his chamber sitting by the fire and talking of his family, his dreams and his desire for revenge. Each day he seemed to improve, as less and less madness gripped his mind and mouth. The pitchers of blood were welcomed and drank seemingly with pleasure. It was time to remove the shackles and see his response to the additional freedom.

Lara entered his chamber and found him sitting at the table waiting for her. She walked across the room and stood in front of him holding a key. "It is time to remove your shackles," she smiled, as she lifted his hand, inserted the key and the cuff fell from his hand. After removing the other hand from its restraint, she placed the key in her pocket and stood quietly waiting for his response.

He stood looking at his hands and then walked about the room shaking them, as if he was putting life back into them. Looking up from his hands to see her beautiful eyes, a tear slowly fell upon his cheek. Quickly turning to face the wall so she would not see, he raised his hand and wiped it from his face as he quietly responded his reply, "Thank you. I longed for this release."

"You have recovered well enough from the madness and need not be restrained within this chamber," she replied.

The nightly knock was heard from the door and Charlotte entered with the evening pitcher. She walked to the table and set it down not noticing that Thomas was no longer restrained. As she turned and stepped toward the door, she saw Thomas standing with his hand upon the door handle. She slowly approached the door and nervously looked at Thomas.

"I must apologize for my behavior toward you. It was wrong of me," Thomas said, as he slightly bowed his head and backed away from the door.

She nodded her acknowledgement. Pulling the door open, she left swiftly through the door locking it immediately. He felt sadness consume his body when he heard her lock the door.

"How long must I stay within this cell?" Thomas asked, as he left the door and approached Lara. "I miss the feel of the night air and the sounds of the trees blowing in the wind. As a farmer, I spent most of my day in the fresh air."

"I hope this will please you," Lara responded with joy in her voice. "Tomorrow we will walk within my private courtyard. You have shown much progress, and it should be rewarded. You will be among humans and other vampires. It may be difficult for you to be with humans, but I am sure you will overcome the temptation."

"I don't want to go back to the monster that I was before you found me," replied Thomas, as he sat down at the table and reached for his cup. "I want to leave that part of my life behind and never think of it again."

"It will do you good to feel the night air," Lara said, as she walked toward the table and placed both hands upon its surface facing him. Leaning forward, she ran her hand across his forehead to move the hair from his eyes. Feeling a slight tingle on her fingertips, she straightened and smiled. "You should be proud. You fought the madness and earned the right to freedom from this chamber. I will leave you to your meal and will make plans for our walk tomorrow evening. You will enjoy the courtyard. It offers a wonderful view of the stars. It always gives me peace."

"I look forward to seeing the stars with you," he replied, as he thought about seeing her more than seeing the stars in the night's sky.

Hearing his thoughts, she smiled and walked toward the door. Placing her hand upon the handle, she blinked making the lock release and opened the door.

"McDuff will bring new clothing to your room and lead you to my courtyard," Lara stated, as she turned to see him once more before she left the chamber. "You will like him. He is a sweet old man."

Lara bid him goodnight and left the chamber pleased with his progress.

* * *

There was a quick rap at the door. As it opened, a large man brought in a copper tub and placed it by the hearth. Two more men carried large pails of steaming water and dumped them into the tub.

"Your bath is ready sir," said the large man. "If you get undressed, I will take your clothes for laundry."

Thomas quickly undressed and stepped into the tub of steaming water. He could feel the heat seep into his muscles, and it felt magnificent. The men left the room as he let his body sink further into the water. This was a luxury compared to the old wooden wash tub his family had used. He had never had a bath in such a fine tub. It was big enough to submerge his whole body into without feeling his knees pressed against his chin.

As the water began to cool, he heard the door open again. This time, a short portly man with very few hairs left atop his head entered the chamber. He carried a stack of clothes and a pair of black leather boots. Walking across the room, he laid them neatly upon the bed.

"I am McDuff. My Lady has sent me here to dress you for the walk in her courtyard this evening," McDuff grinned from ear to ear as he waited for Thomas to approach him.

Thomas climbed from the tub and dried himself with the large cloths that were left on the stool beside the tub. He could sense that McDuff was a vampire and appeared to be a happy soul. Once dressed, McDuff eyed him up and down and clapped his hands together as a child would do upon seeing something special.

"You are ready and will look quite handsome with My Lady to-night. I will escort you to the courtyard. Are you ready to leave this chamber?" McDuff asked with much enthusiasm.

"I am more than I can say. Thank you McDuff, for your help," Thomas replied with sincerity in his voice. "I cannot wait to feel the night air and see the stars."

I cannot wait to see Lara!

They climbed the many stone steps and strode through the dim hallways until they reached the doorway to the courtyard. Opening the door, he could see her sitting by the fountain waiting for him. The blue brocade of her gown matched her eyes and highlighted her strawberry blonde curls that hung about her shoulders. He walked toward her without noticing the guards stationed around the courtyard. She looked beautiful, and he couldn't pull his gaze from her eyes that spar-kled in the moonlight. She stood up as he came closer, and she reached out her hand for him to take.

"I am so happy you could join me here tonight. It is nice to be able to see you outside of the chamber," she said, as she turned slightly to put her arm through his. Feeling a slight tingle of something electric warming her body, she smiled enjoying the warmth. They walked slow-ly for a time without talking. Lara stopped at a table that was elegantly dressed with two chairs and motioned to take a seat. He pulled the chair out for her and helped her sit comfortably. He then took the seat across from her.

She is the most beautiful woman I have ever seen. I cannot believe what has happened to me.

Charlotte approached the table carrying a crystal decanter and two crystal cups that rested within pewter bases engraved with flowers and leaves. She sat the gleaming crystal down on the table and filled each cup with a burgundy liquid that smelled of ripe berries. Leaving the decanter on the table, she quietly left and moved into the shadows.

"To your recovery and a very long future," Lara exclaimed, as she raised her cup to Thomas. She watched his smile travel to his silver-gray eyes.

He raised his cup in return and replied, "To you, for saving me!" They took a sip from their cups. As Thomas sat his cup upon the ta-ble, he said, "I will never be able to repay you for the kindness you have shown me."

"Are you interested in staying here at the castle?" Lara asked. Hoping he would say yes, she took another sip of sweet wine.

"It would be an honor to serve you," replied Thomas with a look of appreciation upon his face.

Charlotte returned with a platter of cheese, bread, fruit and slices of meat. She placed it on the table and returned to the shadows.

"It has been some time since I have eaten food," sighed Thomas, as he watched Lara serve a portion of each item on a pewter plate and set it before him. "It is important to nourish our body with human food. We do this to maintain a link to our humanity," replied Lara. "Our body becomes weak and beckons the madness if we do not keep it strong."

After their meal, they gazed at the stars and talked for hours. Soon, the darkness began to fade and the courtyard began to brighten with the rise of the morning sun.

"It appears to be time to return to our chambers," responded Lara. Thomas stood and pulled the chair back as Lara stood and stepped from the table. "I have enjoyed the evening very much and hope that you were not too uncomfortable. It is sometimes difficult to keep the madness away."

"The evening was wonderful, and I hope that I may have the pleasure of your company again soon," Thomas replied, as he nervously awaited her response.

"I believe that can easily be arranged," Lara spoke softly while taking the arm of Thomas and feeling the same warm tingle she felt before. They walked slowly as she led him toward the courtyard door. "I have made arrangements for you to be moved to more desirable quarters. McDuff will show you the way."

Hearing the door open, McDuff stepped into the courtyard. "Are you ready to retire to your new chamber, Sir?" McDuff asked in a respectful tone.

Turning toward Lara and taking her hand, Thomas bent slightly and softly kissed the back of her hand sending an unexpected rush of warmth through her body and his. "Thank you for an enjoyable evening," responded Thomas. He straightened and looked into Lara's eyes to see if she had felt the same sensation. She smiled and lowered her eyes as she gently pulled her hand from his grasp. She watched him turn and leave through the door without looking back.

What was that? Have I finally found him? Can this be the one I have waited for all these years, she thought to herself holding her hand against her chest?

She took a moment to listen to his thoughts as he left for his chamber. He was happy, and he was thinking of her which pleased her very much.

* * *

McDuff opened the large wooden door and stepped through to the chamber holding the door open for Thomas to enter. It was far grander than anything he had ever seen. As McDuff walked across the room to close the shutters, Thomas stepped about the large room taking in all of the rich wood paneling and hand carved furniture.

"This is much too grand for me, McDuff. I am a farmer and have no royal blood warranting this chamber," stated Thomas, as he stood looking to see if McDuff had made a mistake and chosen the wrong chamber.

"My Lady has chosen this chamber for you. Her chamber is at the end of this hallway and she wants you near," explained McDuff, as he smiled his usual happy smile. "There are bed clothes in the chest, if you desire them, and your bathing room is through the door behind the leather chair." He moved to the bed and began to turn down the bed covers and ready the bed for the daylight hour. "A few personal belongings were found on you when My Lady brought you to Evergreen Castle. I removed them and put them in the small wooden chest by the bed." He watched as Thomas glanced at the wooden chest that held all of his worldly belongings. "Is there anything else you require before I leave you to rest?"

"No, you have been very helpful, and I think I can take care of the rest of my needs by myself," replied Thomas, as he sat down in the chair and started removing his boots. He glanced at the stone floor and noticed the colored beams of daylight starting to seep through the stained glass windows on either side of the shuttered window. He knew it was time to rest, but he couldn't stop thinking about all he had been through.

It was Lara's help that had gotten him through the madness, and a debt that he could never repay in full. She was strong, amazing, and the most beautiful woman he had ever seen. The more he thought of her, the more he wanted to be near her. He wondered where she was and what she was doing. Feeling his eyes begin to burn and his vision begin to change, a blurry scene appeared. As it cleared and came into focus, it provided a glimpse of a large bed chamber with ivory bed linens and deep blue velvet window coverings. Surprised, he shook his head, and the vision was gone.

I must really need sleep, he thought. I am starting to hallucinate.

He stood and stripped off his tunic and breeches. Leaving them in a pile on the floor, he walked over to the bed and sat down on its edge. Studying the wooden chest, he paused before he opened it fearing what memories might consume him. Lifting the lid, he could see something gold resting against the dark velvet interior. As he retrieved the item, a gold chain slipped from his fingers and hung over the side of his hand. It was his mother's locket, and the chain had been broken. His father had presented it to her on their wedding day. It was engraved with a tree and held tiny locks of her children's hair. She never removed it from her neck. He had found it in her apron pocket when he prepared her for burial. He assumed it had fallen into her pocket during the struggle and gone unnoticed by her murderers. Looking again into the chest, he saw his dagger given to him by his father upon his sixteenth birthday. It was a simple dagger with a leather wrapped hilt. Picking up the dagger, he rubbed his hand across the blade.

I will use this dagger to end the lives of those that murdered my family.

Inspecting the inside of the chest to see if anything else was inside, he saw a piece of rolled parchment tied with a thin cord. Placing the dagger upon the table beside the bed, he retrieved the parchment and untied the cord. He found a sheet of music with lyrics his sister's had written as a gift to their mother for her birthday. This had been among the remains of the cottage, and he must have put it in his vest for safe keeping. It wasn't much, but it was all he had left to help him remember his family. He put the items back into the chest and closed the lid. Rubbing his hands through his hair and wondering what the next evening would bring, he laid himself back against the large feather pillows and closed his eyes. Sleep was upon him quickly.

Chapter 2

Lara woke to the sound of Flora's skirt softly rustling as she entered her bed chamber. She had served Lara for almost a century and had become a trusted confidant. Her long brown hair hung to her waist in soft ringlets, and they bounced as she walked across the stone floor toward the bathing chamber. She began to remove the scented oils from the cupboard when Camilla and Caprice entered the room carrying pails of fresh water. After pouring the water into the copper tub, they made their way to the window pulling back the heavy blue velvet window coverings revealing the moon that hung like a slice of melon in the sky. Caprice pulled the doors open from the large hand carved armoire, and Camilla removed the clothing Lara would need for the evening. Flora reached into the water and began to swirl the water with her hand. As the water moved gently in a circle it began to heat. Once it was warm enough, she withdrew her hand and picked up the decanters of bath oil.

"My Lady, your bath is ready," Flora said, as she beckoned Lara to rise from her bed. She poured Lara's favorite lemon and mint bath oil into the water and swirled it once more with her hand.

Lara sat up and pushed back the ivory satin bed linens. She slid her legs over the side of the bed and slipped her feet into the velvet slippers waiting for her.

"Good evening, My Lady," spoke Camilla and Caprice at the same time as they bowed slightly.

"Good evening to you," replied Lara smiling. "Camilla, please ask McDuff to ready Thomas for the evening. I would like to meet with him in the library."

"Yes, My Lady," she replied, as she hung the emerald green brocade dress upon the brass hook of the armoire and headed toward the door.

While stretching her arms as she headed toward the bath, Lara's thoughts drifted back to Thomas. He had been on her mind first thing upon waking, and she hoped that he might be thinking of her too. It would be so easy to invade his thoughts, but she felt the need to respect his privacy. As she stepped into the tub and sank down into the warm water, she closed her eyes and inhaled the fragrance of lemon and mint. She would normally linger in the bath, but this evening she was anxious to see Thomas again.

* * *

Thomas paced back and forth as he waited for Lara. He looked around the library noticing the vast number of books and scrolls. The bindings on most were worn, reflecting their use over the years. Titles of many of the books were in languages he had never seen before, and it made him wonder about the interesting passages they might contain. Against the wall resting under a large map, a wood and iron table was stacked high with yellowing parchments. The ink well and quill rested upon a blank parchment, as if they were waiting for someone to start writing.

I wonder how long it would take to read all of these books, he thought, as he sat down on the leather chair trying to still his nerves.

He heard the sound of footsteps shortly before the door opened and Lara made her way into the room. He stood and bowed his head slightly as she approached. "You wished to see me, My Lady," stated Thomas, as he straightened.

"Yes, did you sleep well?" asked Lara. Feeling a little nervous, she grasped her hands together to keep them from shaking.

"I did," he responded. "I found the chamber much grander than I am warranted, but it offered much comfort."

With concern in her voice she asked, "How is your need to feed? Do you find it difficult to deal with the animal blood?"

"It will take some getting used to, but it is a relief to find the madness gone from my mind," he answered with the sound of relief in his voice.

"The madness is never completely gone. It will always be there waiting to take hold of you again. I myself must work to control the desire for human blood, and I have dealt with this for a very long time," she responded with a sympathetic tone.

"Please sit," she offered her hand toward the chair across from her as she sat down smoothing the folds from her skirt. "I wanted to speak to you about what you might do now that you are here at Evergreen Castle. Do you have a desire to continue the farming you performed before coming here, or might you prefer to learn the skills of the army? It would be your choice to make," she asked, as she looked into his silver-gray eyes.

"I would hope to put farming in my past and do something worthy of helping or protecting others," he responded, nervously moving his hands about as he spoke.

"Good! I hoped for this answer. I have asked Preston, my Army Commander, to show you the Command Center and explain the work that we do here in Evergreen Castle and the surrounding villages. I thought you might find this interesting. He will be here shortly," Lara stood as if she heard something in the distance. "He will also assist with your exercise training."

A knock at the door interrupted Thomas' attempt at responding his acceptance. As Thomas stood, the door opened and in walked a tall muscular man with a full beard of reddish brown. He bowed toward Lara and raised his right hand over his heart.

"Preston, this is Thomas. Please show him the Command Center and get him started with the training exercises. I'm sure Baxter and Elda will enjoy working with a new recruit," she turned to Thomas smiling. She moved her hand in Preston's direction letting Thomas know that he should follow him. "I will expect a report on his progress and any special skills or powers that are discovered. He is newly turned, and it has not been determined if any exist."

Following Preston's lead, Thomas bowed slightly and left through the door, closing it behind him.

* * *

Looking up, Baxter saw Preston entering the exercise room followed by a vampire he had never seen. Hearing Preston going over the responsibilities of the army, he waited until he was called forward to meet the vampire. Baxter was human and had diligently worked his way up through the Evergreen Army. He was tall and had a strong lean frame that allowed him to wield a sword as good as anyone at the castle, vampire included. His light blonde hair hung to his shoulders and his attempts to maintain a beard was the topic of much of the teasing he received from the other men.

Seeing Preston signal for him, he put down the staff and met them in the middle of the room. "Baxter, this is Thomas. My Lady has asked that he start his training. He is newly turned and there is no knowledge of any powers that may have been gifted to him. I put him in your charge to evaluate his abilities," Preston stated with authority.

"Yes sir. I will assign Jario and Elda to start working with him. Elda is good at drawing out special powers," replied Baxter, as he wiggled his eyebrows at Thomas.

As Preston started to walk away, he turned to address Thomas. "We do our best around Evergreen Castle, and My Lady expects nothing less. Vampire or human does not matter to her. Work hard and it will be rewarded," he said with a stern look upon his face and then nodded to Baxter and turned to leave.

Baxter smiled and slapped Thomas on the shoulder as he offered his hand he said, "Welcome to the Evergreen Army. First let's get you in some clothes that you can work in and see what you can do." Following Baxter into a side room he watched as Baxter rummaged through breeches and tunics, pulling out what appeared to fit Thomas. Baxter handed the clothing to Thomas, "Change into these and come back out, and we will get started."

Walking back into the exercise room in his army apparel, Thomas noticed a man and woman entering through a side door and joining Baxter.

"Thomas, come meet Jario and Elda. They will be your instructors during your training," shouted Baxter, as he watched Thomas hurry towards them. "Jario, Elda, this is Thomas. Give him a good work session today to establish his strength and ability with weapons. Let me know about any powers that you discover. Report to me when the tests are complete." Looking at Thomas, Baxter grinned. "They will not go easy on you. You are here to learn to defend yourself and Evergreen Castle."

Nodding at Baxter, he watched as Elda extended her hand. Shaking her hand, he then extended his hand to Jario. In turn, Jario shook his hand firmly and handed him a dagger. "Elda, give him a lesson," Jario smirked. "I will grade his abilities."

I see Lady Lara has taken pity on another stray vampire, Jario thought, as he looked Thomas up and down. She brings these poor souls in and cares for them like they are lost dogs. One of these days she is going to fall for one of them. I intend to prevent that from happening. I intend for her to be mine.

Chapter 3

Lara made the rounds through the castle as she often did checking on the health of her people. She had looked in on Woodward, a human and the forest warden, and found the stores were full of meat and blood. He was an excellent hunter and never took more from the forest than he needed. He often brought back an animal that had lost its mother and cared for it until it could be released back into the forest.

She noticed that Charlotte was standing in the kitchen at the large wooden table covered with vegetables she had gathered during the morning. Her tiny frame, fair complexion and hair made her look fragile, but she was strong in body and mind. Lara sensed her daydreaming again of Woodward. Reading her thoughts, she smiled and secretly wished they would become mates. They were both sweet souls and too shy to approach each other. Charlotte loved her work at the castle and took good care of the pantry spending her free time outside in the garden. With Flora's gift of making plants grow, she kept the garden thriving with plenty of produce.

Making her way to the stone steps that led to the tower, she carefully climbed the many steps to visit with the witch, Meadow, who lived in one of the tall towers of the castle. Lara had found her abandoned when she was just a small child and brought her to the castle giving her the name Meadow, from the place where she was found. It was not made clear that she was a witch until she reached the age of sixteen. Strange things began to transpire causing anxiety for many of the people living in the castle. As Meadow grew, she enjoyed watching the old witch, Ida, which lived within the tower. Seeing her curiosity, Ida tested Meadow and determined that she was truly a witch and began to tenderly teach her the ways of white magic.

Years later, confident that Meadow was obedient to white magic and faithful to Lady Lara, the old witch began to tire of her life. She missed the comfort of her sisters that had passed on years ago leaving her alone. Ida decided it was time to leave her earthly home and Lady

Lara behind. It was time to enter the otherworld, to join her sisters.

One evening when the moon was full and the stars were scattered brightly in the sky, she said her goodbyes to Lady Lara and Meadow. Ida left the castle making her way to the Hill of Entrance set far above Evergreen Castle. Reaching the stone pillar erected by the people to honor the kindness of the White Witches, she knelt down, bowed her head placing her hands on her heart and whispered a few words before she vanished in a wisp of white sparkling mist that ascended to the stars.

Before Lara could knock on the door, it opened revealing Meadow sitting by the fire reading an old leather bound book which floated just above her lap. Meadow was a tiny woman. Her eyes were as green as the moss that grew on the rocks. Her hair was the color of ripe golden apricots and wild as lightening. Her hair never seemed to rest at her shoulders, but flew above her head, as if she constantly stood in the wind. She kept to herself and busy reading her books and collecting herbs for spells.

"Come in My Lady," she greeted Lara with a smile. "Tell me the news of the castle." Lara knew that the witch already knew everything that went on within the castle, and she just wanted the conversation.

"We have a new vampire," Lara replied, as she sat across from Meadow. "I would like you to read him for me."

Meadow gave her a quizzical look as she asked, "Do you want to ask me anything else while you are here?" Meadow smiled and tilted her head to show she knew there was something else on the Lara's mind.

Lara's hands fidgeted within her lap as she spoke, "Yes, something strange has happened. Something I have never felt before. Can you explain what it means? Is he the one I have waited for all this time?"

Meadow smiled and replied, "I can read him if you like, but I have already seen his coming and know that his courage will be severely tested. Whether he passes or fails is unknown to me. The outcome is based on his free will to decide what action he will take. I have determined his powers are weak, and they need to be exercised for they are important to Evergreen Castle. If he fails his test, his powers will be lost and your people will suffer. If he passes his test, greatness will befall all at the castle and you will have a mate for all eternity. This is all I have seen. I can tell you no more."

Hearing that Thomas was her intended mate, she was overwhelmed. This was such good news, but the test of his courage was a mystery. Concern filled her chest as she thought of her people and how they would suffer if he failed. She had to make sure that whatever his test was, he would succeed. Thanking Meadow for her vision, Lara bid her good evening and headed for the stables to check on Mona.

* * *

Jario had been watching Elda sparring with Thomas for hours. He stood leaning against the wall in the corner of the room. Even though Thomas was spending more time on his backside than standing, he was beginning to anticipate her moves and occasionally defend himself.

"I can see that you have this well in hand," spoke Jario to Elda. "I'll leave you two alone so you can finish the session. I have other things that I can be doing." Jario smirked while he ignored the disgusting look Elda gave him and turned and walked away.

After leaving the training session with Thomas, Jario made his way to the stables in hopes of seeing Lara. She often visited the white mare, Mona, that was due to foal and had been separated from the other horses. She had raised Mona from birth and was now anxiously awaiting her foal to arrive. As he opened the door to the stables, he saw her open the gate and enter Mona's stall. He could hear the horse moving around the stall and her softly trying to calm her. Jario quietly made his way through the stable and looked through the slats of the gate.

Suddenly, Mona became agitated at the sight of Jario. "Why are you here Jario? You are obviously causing Mona great anxiety," Lara spoke, with anger in her voice as she stroked Mona's neck trying to calm her.

"I meant no harm. I came to see if you needed help with the mare. She is close to her time, and I thought I could be of service," he responded.

"I think it best you leave," Lara replied, as she tried to calm Mona by stroking her nose. "She seems uncomfortable with you here."

Jario backed away from the gate of the stall. He didn't care about the mare, he just wanted to see Lara. It was hard to keep his desire for her under control. He knew that she could read his thoughts, and he tried to keep his mind clear when he was around her.

"I will leave you now," he said. "If you need my help with the birth, please send for me." He walked away trying to hide his thoughts of anger. It did not matter what he did, she ignored his advances.

* * *

Back in his chamber he growled and cursed as he sat down to re-move his heavy black boots. One at a time, he threw them against the stone wall and watched them fall to the stone floor. Leaning back against the soft leather of the chair, he grabbed his head with both hands and closed his eyes as if that would give him relief. Jario's mus-cular frame filled the chair, and he knew he was bigger and stronger than most of the men in the army. He couldn't understand why she was not attracted to him. He knew he was handsome enough. He of-ten heard Magna say that he was dangerously handsome with his short hair, trimmed beard, and blue eyes that drove her crazy. Sensing his arousal with a single thought of Magna, he quickly turned his thoughts back to Lara and his current problem.

There was always something that interfered with him spending time with her. Now that this new vampire had entered the castle and was requiring his time in the exercise room, he had even less time to get close to her. He had to figure out a way to spend more time with her. He had to make her think that he was in love with her. It would take great acting on his part to accomplish this, but he would and could do it to gain control of Evergreen. With Evergreen came power, and it was all about the power for him.

The castle is really what I want, but the only way to get it is through mating with Lady Lara and becoming Lord Jario. If I can't have her, no one else will have her either. I will make sure of it.

Slamming his fists down against the carved arms of the chair, he felt his anger flare. He stood and removed his remaining clothing dropping them to the floor and kicking them out of his way as he walked naked to the window. Drawing the shade back, he could see the warm glow of the flickering lanterns in Echo Bluff off in the dis-tance.

It was a small waterway village filled with farmers and fisherman. The village had gotten its name from the steep cliffs along the water and the way the sound of the waves echoed against the rocky bluff. Tales of vicious mermaids in the harbor had been told for years, but no one had actually seen them. Many a crew member went missing late at night prompting the tales to continue. The harbor offered a chance to sell goods from the village and take on supplies. The village provid-ed the ship's crew food, ale and a chance to blow off steam. It brought coin to the small village which they greatly appreciated, even though, the crew were generally wild and sometimes abusive.

It had been some time since Jario had consumed the strong taste of ale, and he longed for an evening of strong ale, easy women and fresh warm blood. Consuming human blood was strictly forbidden under promise of imprisonment. It was against Lady Lara's one and only rule, but Jario was clever and had bargained with a nearby witch to hide the proof of his addiction. Anxious for the feel of a woman beneath him and his fangs in her neck, Jario dressed quickly and headed out of the castle for the tavern.

Chapter 4

Yelling and screaming could be heard from outside the old tavern. Swinging the door open, Jario could see that the ship had docked in the harbor and brought many of its crew members to the tavern. He smiled and knew that this offered even more of an opportunity for blood. It was the sweet blood of a woman that he preferred, but a man's blood would suffice. Once they were drunk enough, they would never remember his fangs. If they happened to die, he could throw them out to sea and everyone would think the mermaids had taken them.

The tavern was filled with the hazy smoke from the burning tobacco of men's pipes and reeked of the harsh scent of body odor. Through the smoke he spotted two vampires he had seen here many times before. He had shared ale, women and killing with them on several occasions.

Gustavo and Buck were regular customers at the tavern. Gustavo was tall, muscular and covered in tattoos. He had the power of wind and could easily fill the sails on a ship, if needed. For this, he had picked up the nickname of Gusty long ago. Buck had skin the color of strong coffee and ears that were filled with golden rings. The rings were rumored to represent the gifts from women of royalty that had willingly followed him to bed. Even though Jario enjoyed listening to Buck brag about his lovemaking skills, he doubted the truth in this tale. He surmised they were probably stolen from pirates that came to port. He grew to enjoy their company, and their cruel sense of adventure excited him.

The men were enjoying a mug of ale and each had a buxom woman sitting on their laps. The women pressed their bodies tightly against the men and helped them tip their mugs to their mouths. Seeing the fun they were having, Jario made his way to the table and pulled out a stool to sit.

"Another round for my friends here," he yelled to Zeb behind the bar.

Nodding slightly, Zeb turned and filled a round of mugs with the amber ale. His wife, Lulu, put them on a tray and brought them to the table. Jario slapped the woman on the rump and grabbed his mug spilling the ale as he brought it to his mouth gulping it down quickly. He felt the slap of Lulu's hand across the back of his head before he could set the mug down on the table.

"Mind your manners," Lulu fussed at Jario. "I'm old enough to be your mother. Show me some respect." She left the table in a huff and everyone laughed.

"I have missed the taste of ale," he barked and raised his mug silently to Zeb, asking for another. "What have you two been up to since the last time I saw you?"

"The usual fun," replied Gusty. "Drinking, stealing coin and playing with beautiful women. As you can see, it is the beautiful women that we enjoy this evening."

Shaking his head, Jario laughed at the waste of their talents. He had hoped to enlist them into his army once he had gained control of Evergreen Castle, but the process was taking a lot longer than he had planned.

Jario heard the door open and inhaled a familiar scent of smoldering coals. Walking through the door was Magna in all her glory. She was the rebellious little sister of Lady Lara and had been deemed an outcast for many decades. Her hair was flame red extending to the back of her knees and her eyes were black as coals. Dressed in skin tight leather breeches, corset, and black leather boots she could easily possess the soul of any man in the tavern, including his own. She frequently dabbled in torture and loved to hear men scream. She was definitely right up his alley and the sight of her excited him.

"Magna," Jario yelled. "Come sit with us. I'm buying tonight."

Magna walked toward the friendly group sitting at the table swaying her hips as she took in the many stares from men about the room. She bent down to kiss Jario exposing her cleavage to him but changed her mind and pulled back at the last moment.

"I'm mad at you, sweet Jario. You have not come to see me, and I hear rumors that you are trying to court my sister," whined Magna, as she sat down on his lap pouting her full lips.

"It is my burden to bear," responded Jario. "I shall have to resolve your unhappiness in some way that will please us both." He signaled again for more ale as he put his arm around Magna. Drawing her body against his, he could feel her breast press against his chest and knew he wanted to feel more of her. "I am here tonight, and I am all yours. You need only ask if you desire to have fun."

More ale arrived at the table while Jario and his friends spoke of blood and power. Becoming bored with the conversation, Jario looked at Magna as he ran his hand down her arm to her elbow and then against her leather breeches. He could feel the leather laces that ran from her waist and down between the curves of her bottom. Licking his lips, he suddenly gasped as he felt her hand move from her thigh to the top of his breeches and against the hair on his abdomen.

"I have many things to tell you and would enjoy discussing them with you when we are alone," Jario grinned, as he nipped at her ear. He could feel his arousal strain against the leather laces of his breeches as her hand softly caressed him.

"There is no time like the present," Magna replied, eagerly grabbing Jario's hand and pulling him toward the door.

He could hear the foul comments from Gusty and Buck as they walked through the tavern and stepped through the door into the night air. Magna looked into Jario's eyes with a wicked smile. Anticipating she would flash, he held her tightly around the waist. She kissed his mouth letting her fangs graze his bottom lip drawing a few drops of blood. Pulling back, she laughed as she licked the blood from her fangs. Stroking his face with the back of her hand, she suddenly winked and they vanished into her tell-tale wisp of red smoke that faded into the night air.

* * *

The old castle built from slabs of black stone found in the Canyon of Obscurity stood in ruins. It was a war among two witches hurling black magic that brought down the walls and turned the land around the castle black growing nothing but poison black thistles. Only one witch survived the war, and she lived in a small cottage hidden within the forest near the castle. Velsa had strong black magic, and she loved to bargain her magic in return for a payment of her choosing and her benefit.

Magna had taken up residence in the dungeon of the castle. It was Jario that had suggested it after Lara had ordered her death for the torture and killing of humans. Since the castle was rumored to be haunted with the souls of those killed during the War of the Witches, visitors were rare. Those that were brave enough to trespass into the castle never found their way home, keeping the rumors alive and Magna safe from the Evergreen Army.

As the red smoke began to vanish, Jario looked about the room to see where Magna had brought him. He wasn't surprised to see the dungeon cells that Magna favored so much. "I see you have plans for this evening," Jario smirked, as he looked about the room lined with dark dirty cells.

Hearing a low whimper, he turned around to find a young woman huddled in the corner cell. She was dirty and sat naked with her knees drawn up to her chin. Her arms were wrapped around her legs, and she trembled from the cold night air. There were bite marks along her arms and thighs that were crusted over with dried blood. The few torches about the dungeon reflected in her eyes filled with tears. He could see dark circles that had formed around her eyes from lack of sleep.

Next to her sprawled on the stone floor was a man lying on his back. His breeches were torn and covered in blood. His tunic was gone and small cuts littered his chest and arms. His face was turned to the side and rested in a small pool of blood that had come from a cut across his cheek. Jario could hear him breathing, but it was so shallow, he doubted he would live through the night.

I see you have been busy," Jario laughed, as he stepped close to the young woman. The woman hid her face out of fear and trembled as he neared her. He inhaled her scent, and his fangs dropped as he felt his desire to feed.

"Jario, I thought you were here to play with me tonight, not with my little pets," Magna whined and gave him her best pouting expression. "If you are good, I'll let her play with us later. For now, I want to play with you. Only you."

Magna pointed to the cell wall and smiled as she took Jario's hand and led him into the largest cell. She picked up the cuff that had chains attached and beckoned him to stand against the cell wall. Willingly, Jario backed against the wall and lifted his arm so that Magna could close the cuff around his wrist. She bent to pick up the other cuff and Jario lifted his other arm so that she could restrain it as well. As she tore open Jario's tunic, she asked him in a wicked whisper, "Shall we play?"

Magna extended her claws and began dragging them down Jario's chest causing him to scream as his skin shredded beneath them. He felt the venom from her claws burn as it entered his body. The slashes in his chest were healing quickly, but the more venom that entered his body, the slower his body would heal and the more pain it would cause. She continued to drag her claws over his chest and abdomen digging deeper and deeper with each motion. She licked the blood that ran from his wounds and tore off her corset to feel his bloody skin against her bare breasts. He knew the torture would go on for hours. If he did not scream for Magna, she would cause more pain and maybe go too far by killing him. She was controlled by the madness and dove deep into it, letting it have her completely.

Hours had passed, and now, Jario could no longer stand. His chest was raw, and the blood dripped from his body onto the stone floor of the cell. Magna released the cuffs from his wrists and moved him to her bed to heal. She washed his wounds and held a cup of blood to his mouth for him to drink. At first, the healing was slow, but as he drank the blood, his wounds began to heal faster.

"Did you get your fill of torture, my sweet Magna?" Jario whispered through his strained vocal cords. "Was I enough for you."

"It was so exhilarating, and the madness held me tightly tonight," responded Magna, as she wiped the blood from her own body. She climbed into bed and pressed her naked body against his, as he put his arm around her pulling her closer. They cared for each other in the moments after the torture was over, but it never lasted beyond those moments. "If you still desire more, we can drain the boy and turn him for fun later," she said, as she snuggled closer to his body. They rested quietly in each other's arms for the evening was not over. There were plans to discuss with Magna and a young man to drain and turn.

Chapter 5

As Thomas lay flat on his back against the sparing mat for what seemed like the hundredth time, Elda offered her hand to help him stand. He took it, feeling mortified over how little he knew about fighting with weapons and protecting himself. He had been a farmer and thought he had acquired strength from working the fields. However, he did not have the knowledge of weapons or how to use them. He could see that it would take a long time and many more exercise sessions to become good at any of it.

"You have a lot to learn," Elda spoke, as she pulled Thomas to his feet. "Don't be discouraged. This is just your first day. It will all come in time."

Elda had always been a vampire as far as she was concerned and had no recollection of her turning. She assumed it had been so horrific that she had wiped it from her memory and had no desire to try and remember the cause. She loved being a vampire and using her gifts and enhancing the skills she had developed over the years. Letting go of her feminine desire for fancy dresses and curls within her hair, she felt more comfortable in the feel of her tunics and breeches. Keeping her rich brown hair short made it easier to keep some Neanderthal from grabbing it during a sparring session. She was a master with weapons, fearless and could hold her own with anyone in the Evergreen Army. Since coming to Evergreen Castle, she had been devoted to Lady Lara and would lay down her life to protect her.

Seeing that Thomas was in need of a rest, Elda asked, "Since none of your powers have shown themselves to me, how about we try to figure out what powers you have been gifted?" Thomas cautiously nodded not knowing what additional abuse he would have to endure to determine a gift.

They walked across the large exercise room and through a doorway leading into a long hallway. He followed Elda for some distance before she stopped in front of an old wooden door with large black metal hinges. She pulled a key from her vest and inserted it into the lock. As she turned the key, he could hear what sounded like children's voices that were filled with excitement.

What have they locked behind this door, he thought, as he stood back in case something came leaping from the open doorway at him?

"This is the Room of Powers," Elda explained. "It contains all the powers that could be gifted to a vampire. We are here to find out what has been gifted to you, however, know that not all vampires are gifted powers. Do not be disappointed if you receive none, because sometimes they come later." She smiled at Thomas seeing the concern upon his face. "The sounds you hear are from the Wispets that protect the Room of Powers. They are guardians of the gifts and take care of the powers and make certain they stay strong." Seeing Thomas' quizzical look, she continued, "Wispets are not prisoners here in this room and can leave through a portal inside the chamber at any time they choose. They come and go, but are always present when the Wispet Queen performs the Gifting Ceremony." Elda took hold of the large elaborate handle and looked at Thomas. "Are you ready to see what gifts you might receive?"

Thomas walked into the small chamber as Elda followed and closed the door. The light in the room was dim for there were only a few small candles burning about the stone walls. Before him was a smooth stone pillar with a flat surface at the top. He could see what appeared to be words chiseled into the top of the stone in a language he did not recognize. Looking about the room, he could see small clear globes lining the wooden shelves and flickering lights darting among them.

A warm light began to glow above the pillar, and an image of a woman began to appear. She was the tiniest thing dressed in a flowing gown of white embroidered with threads of green and lavender. The emerald green of her eyes were sprinkled with flecks of gold, and her lavender hair danced merrily about her shoulders. Sparkling gems incrusted her forehead like a crown resting above her eyes.

"Step forward Thomas," she spoke softly. "Step forward and place your hands upon the pillar."

Thomas looked at Elda waiting for reassurance. She nodded, and he stepped forward and placed his hands nervously upon the flat surface of the pillar. As he did, the pillar began to warm beneath his hands. The globes about the room began to glow, as three globes moved to the surface of the pillar. They huddled tightly next to each other. A faint sound of chatter and laughter could be heard about the room as the Wispet Queen brought her finger to her mouth to hush the noise. As the room became quiet, he watched as she touched the first clear globe, and it turned the color of the sky during a warm summer. A word that he could not read appeared above the surface of the pillar. "Vision," she said, as the word disappeared and the globe's light faded. She touched the next globe lightly, and it began to brighten to the color of the evergreens about the castle. Again, a word floated above the pillar. "Compulsion," she announced, as he watched the word disappear into the globe and then shake upon the pillar until she gently stroked the top of the globe. As she touched the last clear globe, it began to brighten. It became so bright he had to close his eyes for fear that he would be blinded. "Walk in Daylight," she said, as he heard a slight sizzle before the light dimmed, and he could finally open his eyes. "These three gifts have been given," declared the Wispet Queen, as she looked directly into Thomas' eyes. "Use them well."

The Wispet Queen faded from view as the chatter and laughter increased for a moment and then diminished, returning the room to dim candlelight. The globes floated into the air and swirled about Thomas' head as if they wanted to play. One by one, they returned to their place upon the shelves. Thomas looked at Elda to see if he was to do anything else.

"We are finished here," spoke Elda.

Feeling the pillar cool beneath his hands, he pulled them away looking again at the inscription on its surface and turning to follow Elda. Leaving the room, Elda locked the door and stood facing Thomas with her hand upon his shoulder.

"I will go make my report, and you may return to your chamber," Elda said. "Get some rest. We will start training with longswords tomorrow."

Thomas nodded and watched Elda turn and walk away. He suddenly shouted, "Elda, what did the inscription on the pillar mean?"

Elda turned and responded, "Keep with Honor - Forfeit with Shame."

* * *

Thomas returned to his chamber exhausted. McDuff was waiting for him with a tub of steaming water. He immediately shed his clothes and stepped into the tub. He had left the exercise session with several large bruises and a swollen jaw. He put his hand to his face to feel the place where Elda had elbowed him a number of times.

"They will heal quickly," McDuff commented. "Not to worry. Your body can take more than that now that you are a vampire. Drinking blood will help the healing process too."

McDuff readied the bed and closed the shutters. After placing a large cloth on the stool next to the tub, McDuff picked up his soiled clothes and headed toward the chamber door.

"Charlotte left you a tray of food and a pitcher of blood on the table. Don't forget to eat," McDuff said, before opening the door.

Thomas raised his arm from the water and waved slightly in acknowledgement as McDuff quietly left the room. Thomas leaned back closing his eyes and thought about the powers he had been gifted. It all seemed so strange to him. He would be able to walk in daylight and not be restricted to the darkness. He then remembered the quick vision of a room he had seen.

Was that the vision power I have been gifted? Can I see things that are not right in front of me?

Rubbing his jaw, he sank below the water for relief. Suddenly he sat up making the water from the tub splash to the floor. These are powers that can be used to protect the Lady Lara and her castle. He decided then that he would work hard to strengthen the gifts and use them to not only protect the castle but to find the murderers of his family and bring them to justice.

Chapter 6

Tolin, the Horse Master, was preparing to feed the horses when he heard a banging noise coming from Mona's stall. He ran to the stall door and saw Mona trying to stand. She had a thin layer of sweat covering her coat and seemed restless as she moved about her stall.

He ran to the kitchen door and yanked it open. "Charlotte, get Lady Lara. The mare is about to foal," yelled Tolin. He let the door slam and ran back to the stables.

Charlotte stopped kneading the bread and wiped the flour from her hands onto her apron as she ran to the library. She had just taken Lady Lara a cup of clover tea and knew she would still be there.

Just before she reached the door, Lara pulled the door open. "What's wrong Charlotte?" Lara asked, seeing a worried look on her face.

"The mare is about to foal," replied Charlotte, gasping as she spoke.

"Get Thomas and tell him to meet me at the stables," she ordered, as she sped down the hallway.

Reaching the stables, she could hear the hoofs of Mona hitting the walls of the stall. Quickly opening the stall door and placing her hands on Mona's side, she stroked her gently letting her know she was there for her.

"We have a problem," shouted Tolin. "See the reddish colored bag protruding from the mare. There is no sign of the foal's feet. The foal will die from lack of oxygen, if we don't get it out quickly."

Thomas entered the stall and could immediately see the problem. The mare knelt down and rolled to her side. Tolin and Thomas knelt down at the rear of the mare.

"The placenta has become detached from the foal," responded Thomas. "We need to open the bag and help the foal out quickly, or I fear it will die."

Tolin tore the red bag open and reached in for the front feet that had just come into view. After guiding the first front foot and then the other, they could see the nose was clearly visible. They both pulled gently with the mare's contractions. The head and finally the rest of the body slipped from the mare.

"He is beautiful," sighed Lara, as she pulled the membrane from the new colt. His coat was black with a blaze of white down the bridge of its nose. Quietly, Mona and the new colt rested side by side, as the three spectators stared in amazement at the beauty of what had just happened.

"Mona, you were wonderful," declared Lara, as she kissed the space between the mare's ears. "You have a beautiful new colt."

The mare started to raise up, and as she stood, the umbilical cord broke separating the mare from her colt. The colt jerked his head up and attempted to stand. Determined, he finally stood on wobbly legs and tried to walk toward his mother. Slowly he made his way to the underside of his mother and began to nurse.

"Do you have a name for the colt?" Thomas asked.

"I think I shall name him Arrow," replied Lara. "He has a beautiful white arrow on his nose."

Thomas smiled, as he watched Lara's hands lovingly run against Mona and gently kiss her nose.

This woman has so much love within her soul, he thought, as he watched her stroke Mona's tired body.

"My Lady," Tolin spoke quietly not to disturb the mare and her new colt. "They are out of danger. I can clean up the stall and should be able to care for their remaining needs." Looking at Thomas, he offered his hand as he spoke, "Thank you for your help, Thomas."

"As a farmer, I have helped with the birth of many animals. It was nice to be of help to you both," Thomas replied reaching out to shake Tolin's hand. "If you need my help, please ask. I love caring for animals."

"I might just do that," responded Tolin. "Thanks again."

Leaving the stables, Lara and Thomas walked slowly back to the side entrance of the castle. "How is your training?" Lara asked, as she turned her head to look at Thomas.

"My first day was full of swelling and bruises," he responded rubbing his jaw. "Elda is strong and knocked me on my backside to many times to count."

Lara laughed and nodded her head acknowledging what he meant. "She can hold her own with the best of them," Lara responded. "She is a dedicated member of the army and of Evergreen Castle. You will learn much from her."

Reaching the side entrance, Thomas took her hand to assist her with the stone steps that led to the door. As he touched her hand, he felt the same electric sensation he had before. He felt Lara's hand twitch slightly and knew she had felt it again too. They stepped through the doorway, and he placed his hand at the small of her back, as they continued to walk through the hallway.

A wisp of red smoke appeared behind the stables as Jario and Magna suddenly appeared. She quickly kissed Jario on the cheek, and in an instant, she had vanished. Jario thought about the long evening. He didn't know why he put up with her. She was definitely crazy, and the pain he endured for her was nothing short of excruciating. It humored her, and he thought he may need her help one day, so he put up with her abuse.

As he walked around the corner of the stable, Jario spotted Lara and Thomas walking back to the castle. He could hear their casual conversation and was furious with the attention that she was showing Thomas. They were becoming much too friendly with one another.

He is nothing but a stray, he thought, as he slammed his hand against the stable wall shattering the wood and watching the shards fall to the ground.

"I'll put a stop to this," Jario said angrily out load. "Lady Lara is mine."

Chapter 7

Time passed quickly for Thomas as he worked hard to perfect his gifted powers. Elda kept him focused, and he accepted her praise, as well as, her constructive criticism. He was starting to believe that he would be able to protect Evergreen Castle and find those responsible for murdering his family.

The visions were getting much easier to call into view. He could not only find humans or vampires, but he could also find objects. Elda made a game of hiding his dagger to see how long it would take him to find it. The amount of time it took him to retrieve it became shorter and shorter.

He had deliberately avoided leaving the shelter of the castle during the daylight hours. The first time Jario pushed him out of the door into the daylight, Thomas covered his face with his hands waiting for the sun to burn them to a crisp. Secretly, Jario hoped that Thomas would burn a slow agonizing death. He was greatly disappointed when Thomas stood, with outstretched arms, taking in the sun's rays without the slightest bit of smoke.

Compulsion was the hardest of the three gifts. Elda had him try, time and time again, to compel her to do anything. Each time he tried, he failed. Lara had accidently walked in on one of these sessions and watched the game Elda was playing. Seeing his frustration, she told Thomas that one of Elda's gifts was blocking compulsion. Thomas raised his eyebrow and gave Elda a wicked glare. Elda smirked and backed up expecting a good kick in the ribs. She liked to tease Thomas, and he was a good sport about it, most of the time.

His daily training sessions with Elda and Jario had come to an end. They had been replaced with evening outings to patrol the surrounding villages. Jario was usually absent from these outings, and Baxter was always willing to step in to take his turn. There had been an increase in the killing of humans, and from all indications, a vampire was the cause. It was up to them to capture the vampire and return him, or her, to the Holding Room. If the vampire was beyond their help, they would protect the village by offering the vampire its final death with a stake.

One evening, Elda, Thomas and Baxter were patrolling the cliffs when the swift movement of a dark figure caught their attention as it moved among the shadows. Seeing it move between the barrels waiting to be loaded onto the ship, they watched as it boarded the ship that had recently docked in the harbor. Making their way down to the docks, Elda led their trio up the ramp of the ship.

"Find it," Elda whispered looking at Thomas. "This could be a vampire or human. Either way, it should not be trying to board the ship this late at night."

He closed his eyes and began to pull his vision. It was much easier now, and it quickly offered him a view of the ship. He searched the ship starting at the bow until he found a dark shape crouched down between two wooden barrels near the stern of the ship.

"It is below deck near the stern of the ship. It is in some kind of storage room with only one door, and it doesn't have a weapon," Thomas responded, as he opened his eyes and looked at Elda for direction.

"Let's get this thing," shouted Elda. Baxter and Thomas followed behind her and were swiftly at the door. "We don't know what this thing can do, so be careful Baxter," whispered Elda. She took hold of the iron handle and pushed the door with her shoulder, as she jumped into the room. Thomas followed right behind her, just in time to see a figure stand and step through the wooden planks of the ship's wall and vanish from the room.

"What was that?" Thomas yelled. "Where did it go?"

Thomas closed his eyes and quickly began to search for the figure. His vision led him to the bow of the ship, and he watched as the figure appeared to leap from the ship to the top of the cliffs. The figure turned and looked back at the ship and then fled. "It is gone," murmured Thomas. "How did it do that? It leapt right off the ship?"

Every evening after the sighting of the dark figure, Thomas was on patrol with either Elda or Baxter to protect the village. More and more humans were being killed. The attacks were happening at night, as well as, during the daylight hours. From the looks of their bodies, it was determined a vampire was the cause and had the power of Walking in Daylight. Thomas was given the assignment to work the daylight hours and try to discover where this dark figure hid itself.

* * *

One afternoon after entering the tavern, Thomas noticed fewer customers than usual sitting about the room. He walked to the bar and gave Zeb a friendly nod. Zeb stepped forward and placed his hands on the wooden bar giving Thomas a big grin.

"Zeb, have you seen any strange folks around lately?" Thomas asked, as he looked over his shoulder. He could see Lulu standing with her hands on her hips while she was giving a customer a scolding.

"Almost all of my customers are strange in one way or another," answered Zeb. "Can you tell me what I should be looking for?"

Thomas leaned forward to whisper his response not wanting to alarm anyone, "We don't have much of a description, but we know he can pass through walls."

Zeb looked surprised even after the things he had seen in the tavern, but passing through walls was a new one, even for him. "I will surely know when I see that happen," Zeb replied, as he pulled off his cap and scratched his bald head.

Thomas looked about the room at the few customers. Recognizing most of them, he thanked Zeb for his time and left the tavern heading for the other small shops that were open during daylight hours. He wanted to warn them of the danger.

* * *

Tired of hearing nothing but talk about the dark figure and how he could walk through walls, Jario left the castle and headed for the forest. He summoned Magna and leaned against a tree while he waited for her to appear. Out of the corner of his eye, he saw something move behind a tree, as if to hide.

"I know you are there," smirked Jario. "I can sense your presence."

The young man stepped from behind the tree to face Jario. His clothes were torn and dirty. He had blood smeared across his face and hands. His eyes were deep red and had a wild look about them. Just when Jario was about to speak, a red wisp of smoke appeared, and Magna stepped forward to greet him. Smiling, she started to reach for Jario's arm when she heard the crushing of leaves from behind her. Turning, she recognized the young man that stood before her.

"Oh, it is you, my pet," responded Magna. "You look dreadful." She stepped closer to the man and shook her head in disgust. "I see the blood upon your face. You must have figured out how to feed all on your own." She laughed at him and turned to focus her desires on Jario.

"I thought we decided not to turn him. You were going to keep him in the cell with the half dead girl for playing, feeding or whatever you do with them," Jario shouted, as he began to pace back and forth in front of Magna.

"I changed my mind," Magna said, not liking the anger in Jario's eyes. "He was too delicious, and I couldn't stop myself."

Magna was careless but this was reckless. Making the connection between the dark figure and the young man, Jario stood frozen in place.

"Is this the dark figure that everyone has been talking about?" Jario grumbled. "He is, isn't he? He has been on a killing spree, and the army is expanding the patrols to find him." Jario stood with his hands clenched at his side. Realizing the danger she had put them in, his anger flared. Grabbing Magna's arm, he shouted at her, "You have foolishly let him escape without training him. By letting him escape, you may lead the patrols right to your door."

"Calm yourself, Jario. He got loose, and I wanted to see if he could find his way back to me," Magna responded with her usual pouting look. "Why are you so upset with me? I'll take him back with me and secure him so that he doesn't bother you again. Will that make you happy?"

She yanked her arm away from Jario. Turning her back on Jario, Magna approached the young man and took hold of his arm. Lowering her eyebrows down over her eyes, she turned around and glared at Jario as she pulled the young man against her body. Jario sensed her anger and was relieved that she was taking the young man back to Black Thistle Castle. He watched with relief as Magna vanished leaving her wisp of red smoke behind.

That woman is going to be the final death of me, Jario thought, as he headed back to Evergreen Castle.

* * *

Returning to the Black Thistle Castle, Magna threw the young man back into his cell. "Stay put this time," Magna snarled at him. "You have brought too much attention to yourself. I don't want the army on my castle steps looking for you or for me. Now let me see, we have to call you something since you are going to be around here for a while. Do you have a name or should I name you?"

The young man stood and turned to face Magna. He searched his mind looking for an answer that he could give her. His thoughts were cloudy and unclear, and he strained to remember his name. Names filtered through his mind, and he struggled to remember what he had been named. Unsure, he responded with a ragged breath, "I think my name is Tate."

"Well Tate, get some rest. I want to play later and you know how tired you get when we play," spoke Magna in her usual evil tone. "Your little friend can join us too." Magna stepped from the cell and closed the heavy door. She slid the metal bar latching the door. Pulling a key from her pocket, she inserted the key and turned it until she heard the lock fall into place. Smiling, she took the ring of keys from the wall and slipped the key onto the ring with the others. Returning the ring to the hook on the wall, she turned to face Tate. "This is your home, Tate. You belong to me." Laughter filled the dungeon as she made her way up the stone steps.

Chapter 8

Woodward and Thomas spent the day hunting game in the forest near the castle. Woodward enjoyed his company during the hunts, and they had become good friends. He knew he was old enough to be Thomas' father and sometimes slipped and called him son. Thomas didn't mind, it made him think about his own father and the good times they had shared.

Woodward had been able to teach him how to use the crossbow, and he had become a master with the weapon in a very short period of time. Two hunters in the forest made the work of keeping the stores full much easier. Since the vampire killings in the daylight hour, Lady Lara ordered Thomas to accompany Woodward on the hunts for his protection. He didn't mind the assignment and looked forward to being outside in the sunlight.

This particular morning, the dew was still fresh on the meadow. They had been tracking a buck for days and always seemed to be a day behind it. Woodward knew all of the favorite grazing spots of the different animals. He felt this was the spot to wait for the return of the buck. It hadn't been here for a few days, and he expected him to return for the fresh grass.

They had been sitting on their backsides for what seemed like hours when a rustle was heard across the meadow. Careful not to make a noise to scare away the animal, Woodward raised slightly to see what they had heard.

"It is a buck, and it is the old one carrying eight points. He is too far away to hit with the crossbow. We'll have to wait until he gets closer. Damn, he is a beautiful buck. It is a shame to kill the animal," Woodward sighed softly.

Suddenly, a ferocious scream could be heard from across the field. Knowing the buck must have been scared away, Thomas stood to find a man running toward the buck that stood frozen in place. At the last second before the man reached the animal, it turned and dashed away out of sight. The man stood watching it flee between the trees of the forest. Appearing to notice something, the man suddenly turned to face them. Looking directly at Thomas and Woodward, he started to run toward them at full speed. Thomas realized this man wasn't human and pulled his dagger from his boot.

"Get behind me Woodward," shouted Thomas, as he took a protective stance in front of his partner. Woodward stepped behind Thomas and readied his crossbow if his help was needed.

The closer the man got, the more familiar he looked to Thomas. When the man was within twenty feet of Thomas, he suddenly stopped. Both men stared directly at each other.

Thomas stood in total shock as he forced the words from his mouth, "Tate, is that you?" He was looking at a half starved man with tattered clothes, slash marks upon his body and fangs that pierced his bottom lip. "Brother! It is me, Thomas," he spoke again stepping slowly toward Tate.

Recognition started to filter through Tate's mind as Thomas got close enough to throw his arms around Tate. He held him tightly against his chest. Tate struggled to free himself from Thomas' arms. He heard him call him brother. The voice was familiar, but he couldn't remember where he had heard it. Names and faces flew through his mind. Little by little, the names and faces attached to one another. Suddenly, he fully realized who was standing before him. He started to weep and tightly embraced his brother in response.

"You need help," Thomas whispered in Tate's ear. "Let me help you." Tate tried to pull away, but Thomas held tight and wouldn't let go. "I know someone that can drive this madness from you. Come with me, Tate. Let me get you help."

Tate nodded and let his body relax in Thomas' arms. Thomas pulled away and grasped Tate's bloody hand. As they began to walk, Tate continued to look at his brother. Thomas stayed between Woodward and Tate. He knew that Tate could attack him at any moment and wanted to protect his friend. Leading Tate back to the castle, the two men walked in silence holding tightly to each other's hand. There was so much that Thomas wanted to tell his brother, but it was more important to keep him calm until Lara could help him with the madness. She had helped him and knew she could help his brother.

Woodward had run ahead to warn Lady Lara of the new vampire. As they approached the castle, Thomas could see that she had come to meet them at the back of the entry hall. She stood smiling, as the two men stepped forward.

"My Lady, this is my brother, Tate," Thomas said, as he looked from Lara to his brother. "He desperately needs your help." He held his brothers hand tightly. Afraid if he let go, he would bolt and be lost forever. Lara slowly stepped closer to Tate.

"Tate, will you let me help you?" Lara asked. "I can show you how to control the madness."

Tate looked up at Lady Lara and started to shake his head. "I am beyond help," he said, as tears ran from his eyes. "I am consumed by the darkness. It has seized me and will not let go of me. I am lost and cannot be helped."

"Let me try to help you," she softly said. "If this pleases you, give me your name and take my hand so that you may come with me." Lara offered her hand to Tate.

Exhausted and afraid he would be tortured, Tate stepped away from her. He tightened the grip around his brother's hand.

Sensing his fear, Thomas nudged him forward saying, "You have nothing to fear. She will help you. You can trust Lady Lara."

Tate started to speak and then looked over at his brother. Seeing Thomas nod his head, he took a step forward toward Lady Lara. "My name is Tate." he said, as he felt defeated, and let his shoulders sag. Keeping his hand within his brother's, he started to raise his other hand and then hesitated. Looking at his brother's pleading expression, he willingly extended his hand. Lara took hold of his thin bloody hand and whispered a few short words. Instantly they vanished.

Chapter 9

Tate had great difficulty letting go of the madness. It seemed as though it had wrapped its wicked force around him completely. Even with the animal blood, he still had to be restrained to keep him from trying to attack anyone that entered the chamber. Meadow had come the first night to offer a spell to hide his powers for everyone's protection. After seeing him disappear through the ship's wall and leap through the air, they were afraid the spelled restraints would not hold him.

Nightmares appeared anytime he closed his eyes and slept, causing him to fight his need for sleep to keep them away. Thomas was afraid that he was beyond help, but Lara assured him that it would just take more time and to be patient. Thomas never left the Holding Chamber and had a cot brought to the room so he could be near his brother.

After hearing Tate scream for hours, his brother finally collapsed to the stone floor and slept. It wasn't long before his nightmares had returned. Tate often mumbled in his sleep but this time his words were clear and shocking.

"Jario," he said, tossing his head from side to side. "Magna." Swinging his arms he uttered, "Kidnap Lara."

Thomas listened carefully as Tate continued to wail and fight with his arms.

"Do not kill the girl," he screamed and finally went silent for a while. Becoming agitated again, Tate moaned and murmured more words that Thomas could not understand. He had heard the stories of Lady Lara's sister, Magna, and he knew that she was dangerous. She had left the castle under penalty of death, and the army had been searching for her for years.

Lara opened the chamber door and noticed Tate was finally sleeping. She looked at Thomas and smiled as she closed the door behind her. Walking over to him, she sat down on the cot next to him as she asked, "How is your brother?" As she waited for his response, she placed her hand over his to comfort him. Thomas looked at her hand

and then looked into her eyes.

"I know you feel that. I feel the same sensation every time we touch. It is clear that you do too," he whispered, for fear of waking Tate.

"I have felt it from the first day I met you in the tavern," she replied.

"I am drawn to you and feel great relief when you are near," he offered nervously. "Please forgive my boldness, but I think of you often."

"I feel the same, Thomas. My day ends and begins with thoughts of you," she replied, as she brought her hand up to stroke above his eye and down the side of his face against the stubble of his beard.

"Stop me, if I have misunderstood your feelings," he spoke softly, as he touched her cheek gently with his other hand and leaned in slowly to brush his lips against hers. Her sweet scent of lemon and mint filled his senses.

She sat still, not moving away, enjoying the new closeness they shared. "I had hoped for this for some time," Lara replied, as she leaned toward him to have the taste of another kiss.

Tate screamed and startled them both, making Lara stand and release Thomas' hand. He was still sleeping but raising his hands and arms in a protective manner.

"He has nightmares and frequently fights something in his sleep," Thomas said with concern in his voice. Seeing her tremble, he took hold of her hand trying to calm her. "He spoke of Jario and Magna before you arrived."

Lara turned with a surprised look and asked with urgency, "What, of Magna?"

Thomas stood and tried to take hold of her other hand to calm her. "He spoke of kidnapping you," Thomas replied. "I'm sorry, I should have told you as soon as you entered the chamber."

Lara fisted her hands and began to pace back and forth across the stone floor. She couldn't believe that Jario was associating with Magna. This made him a traitor. She thought he was a faithful member of the castle, and he had sworn his protection to all. Knowing that he was somehow involved with Magna, her devious sister, made it so much worse. Their powers united together could be the castle's undoing. The council needed to be called, but it had to be done without Jario's knowledge.

"I have to inform the council. Jario needs to be arrested," she said, as she held her hands to her face. Worry filled her thoughts. "I have to make sure Evergreen is protected."

Thomas walked her to the door and wrapped his arms around her. "We will figure this out. I promise you. I won't let anyone harm you or Evergreen," Thomas whispered, as he kissed her cheek inhaling her scent once more. Opening the door, he watched her hurry down the hallway out of sight.

As he turned from the door, he noticed that Tate was awake. His eyes were no longer completely red. The bright blue eyes rimmed in black that he remembered were now blue but rimmed in bright red.

This had to be a good sign, he thought.

Thomas approached the table and asked his brother, "Can you talk?"

Tate looked at his brother and held up his hands shaking the chains. "I have gone from one prison to another," he laughed and sighed with disgust. "Torture still finds me when I sleep. I cannot hide from it."

"I understand your frustration, brother. I was held in the same chains until the madness left me," Thomas replied, as he motioned to Tate to come sit at the table. He sat on the wooden stool and waited for Tate to comply.

Tate moved slowly to the table. Picking up the stool, he banged it on the floor before he sat with a grunt. Realizing for the first time that his brother was a vampire, he asked Thomas, "How did you become turned?"

Thomas told him the story of finding their parents and sisters murdered. He tried to explain the grief he felt and the way he left the tavern drunk, night after night, to deaden the pain. He described how the tall man with silver hair had turned him. He told him of how he awoke alone and had to survive on his own, causing him to probably kill more humans than he remembered. He described the night Lady Lara had stopped him from killing a young woman in a muddy alley and brought him to the castle, to help him drive the madness from his body.

Tate listened to his story and felt the pain enter his mind. It wasn't the madness he felt, but the grief of knowing his family was dead. Tears came slowly, and he let them fall as he thought about never seeing his family again.

Thomas reached across the table to take his brother's hand but Tate pulled it back and put it in his lap. "The monster hasn't left me yet," he said, through his tears. "I don't want to hurt you. I don't want to ever hurt you or anyone again. Promise me that when the madness is gone and I am no longer a threat to you or anyone else, that you will let me help you find the murderers of our family."

Thomas stood and put his hand over his chest and said, "I promise you." Tate stood and placed his hand over his chest as Thomas had done. Tate was coming back. It was happening slowly, but it was happening.

Chapter 10

Lara stood calmly before her council and voiced her concerns regarding the words spoken by Tate. The council members listened carefully, but they felt the need to be cautious. Since Tate was still feeling the powerful hold of the madness, they could not be sure his outbursts were true. After much discussion, it was determined that more information was needed before Jario could be questioned. If it were just the ramblings of the madness and nothing else, it would save the council from false charges against Jario. The council wanted to question the young man and draw their own conclusions. Since Tate was still weak, the questions would have to wait. It was agreed by all that they would wait until assurances could be made that he was free of madness and could answer any questions the council might ask.

Lara was in agreement with the council, for now. She was frustrated because Jario was still free to roam about the castle and put her and others in danger. Even though Lara had fighting skills and powers that she could use to defend herself, it was the responsibility of the army to protect her. Preston ordered Elda to act as Lady Lara's security guard until this issue was resolved. Meadow would be called upon to render a spell to prevent Jario or Magna from taking Lady Lara from the Evergreen Castle and surrounding property.

It was important to act as if nothing was different and not to cause Jario to suspect that anyone knew of his dealings with Magna. Lara was surprised that she had not seen anything in his thoughts that would have given him away, but she had not seen him since he visited the stable.

"He hasn't been around much," offered Elda. "He rarely comes to training sessions, and I have seen him leave the castle frequently on foot."

The council was aware of Jario's powers. They were some of the most dangerous powers that could be gifted. Until proven otherwise, he was now considered dangerous to Evergreen Castle.

"He has the power of haze which could hide him when he is around others and could easily allow him to spy on any of us. Keep your senses sharp until this is resolved," ordered Preston.

"Magna knows she is forbidden to return to Evergreen Castle. I would know if she entered the castle. If she stayed more than a few moments, I would feel it," said Lara. "She also leaves a trail of red smoke when she comes and goes. This could easily give her away."

Feeling they were as ready as they could be without getting answers from Tate, the council left the chamber. Lara walked back to the tower with Meadow at her side. Elda followed closely behind them. Once inside Meadow's chambers, Elda took her place outside the door on guard.

Meadow immediately went to her large book of spells and turned the aged parchment pages one by one, as she looked for a spell that would protect her mistress. Lara heard sighs and huffs as Meadow searched through the spells in her book.

Meadow pointed her finger at a page and said, "Finally, this will do!"

Beckoning Lady Lara to stand within the pentagram that was painted on the floor in front of the hearth, Meadow showed her where to stand. She helped her remove her dress to keep the flames of the candles away from her clothing. Removing her slippers and handing them to Meadow, Lara stepped inside of the pentagram. As Lara stood in its center in nothing but her under garments, Meadow carefully placed white candles at each point.

"Be very still and do not make a sound," ordered Meadow with a serious look upon her face.

Meadow waved her hand in a circle and one by one the candles held a small flame. She stood facing Lady Lara and began to chant. The candles began to flicker and tall flames reached the height of Lady Lara's waist. Standing very still, she watched the sparks fly around Meadows body as she swayed and held her eyes closed reciting the words to the spell.

Goddess of Light and Goodness hear my plea,
Protection we ask for this one before me.
An enemy comes knocking to steal her away,
Keep her from leaving by night and by day.
Jario and Magna of this plot are accused,
Block them from leaving their deed be refused.
Goddess of Light and Goodness hear our plea.
Goddess of Light and Goodness we praise thee.

The flames turned white and slowly retreated back to a small flicker. Instantly the flames were gone and a small trail of white smoke left each candle and swirled above Lara's head. They hovered for a moment longer and then vanished. Meadow opened her eyes and smiled.

"It is done," spoke Meadow in a quiet but reassuring voice. "You are protected from Jario and Magna. They cannot take you from the castle."

Lara stepped from the pentagram careful not to step on the lines. Meadow picked up her clothing and helped her step into her dress and draw the laces at her back. Stepping into her slippers, Lara looked up at Meadow and responded, "Thank you for your faithful service."

Meadow nodded in acceptance and slowly returned to her chair and picked up a book that had been turned over to save the spot. She put her hands in her lap as the book floated above her hands.

"Good evening My Lady," Meadow responded and focused her attention on the book in front of her.

"Good evening my lovely Meadow," Lara replied, as she opened the door and closed it behind her.

Chapter 11

Time passed slowly for Tate as he struggled to conquer the madness and deal with remembering what had happened to him. He sat with Thomas every night and told him the things that flashed in his mind. The nights of torture he described receiving from Magna were disturbing. He had watched as Magna and Jario drank from the young woman that had shared his cell. Magna eventually forced Tate to drink from the young woman, and he had helped hold her down as Magna abused her body.

Lara visited the Holding Room often. She was anxious to get any information she could from Tate. Thomas had passed on everything he had learned from his brother, but Tate still wasn't strong enough to sit before the council. Thomas worried that Jario or Magna might make a move to kidnap Lady Lara before the necessary information could be retrieved from Tate.

One evening Lara entered the chamber bringing a tray of food. She motioned for Thomas and Tate to come sit with her at the table. As she served the food she watched Tate closely. He had almost lost the redness in his eyes.

"Tate, how are you feeling," asked Lara, as she continued to place food upon their plates.

"I feel better each day, but the nightmares still haunt me," he responded, not making eye contact with Lara.

"I wonder if I might sit with you this evening," Lara asked, as she glanced at Thomas. "Thomas hasn't been seen around the castle or in the training room since you arrived, and I am afraid that Jario might start asking questions. If he knows there is a new vampire in the castle, he might suspect it is the one he saw in the dungeon. He would know he could be recognized."

Thomas nodded his agreement with Lara. He knew he felt weak from the lack of practicing his powers and training sessions with the army. It was agreed that Lara would sit with Tate for a few evenings. This would allow Thomas to work around the castle and partake in scouting missions as he had been doing before Tate arrived. Thomas gave his brother a reassuring slap on the shoulder and headed toward the door. He turned and gave Lara a wink and left for the training room.

* * *

Thomas could hear the loud clang of the blades from the hallway outside of the training room. He knew Elda was guarding Lady Lara, so it had to be either Baxter training someone or working his own skills with Preston. As he entered the room he could see Baxter and Preston working with longswords. They were both bare chested and sweat dripped from their bodies. He loved the feel of the hilt of the sword within his hands and couldn't wait to get in on the practice.

"Can I cut in?" Thomas asked, bending down to pick up a sword laughing slightly over his use of words.

"Take my place," answered Preston. "I have rounds to make, and Baxter needs the practice."

Baxter took the teasing well and waited for Thomas to get into position. "Are you ready to suffer from the blade of my sword?" Baxter asked Thomas, as he pointed the sword toward his neck.

"Give me everything you've got, my friend," responded Thomas, as he raised his sword and prepared to strike.

The two men gave each other a nod, and their swords began to sing. Thomas' blade came to life and countered every stroke of Baxter's blade. His energy felt heightened, and he was able to anticipate every move that Baxter made. The feel of the hilt within his hand made his arm and blade seem to move as one.

Thomas could hear the door open and close, but he kept his eyes on Baxter's blade. He could hear the sound of boots walking across the stone floor, and he knew the sound of those boots. They were Jario's boots. The boots of a traitor.

Jario walked into the training room and stood watching Thomas and Baxter wielding their swords. Seeing Jario walking toward them, Baxter stepped back from Thomas and yelled, "Jario, why haven't we seen your ass lately? You have missed out on all this entertainment of watching Thomas attempt to wield his sword."

Trying to ignore Baxter, Jario smirked and gave Thomas a hateful look. "I've been busy," replied Jario in a nasty tone. Out of frustration, he ran his fingers down over his face and neck. "I've been watching the village and the new ship that docked in the harbor. I don't have time to spend teaching Thomas the skills of a sword. From the looks of it, Thomas has become your equal. Maybe, it is you that I should be teaching." Jario smirked, before turning his back on the men. He stormed across the room leaving through the door to the hallway.

He hasn't noticed I have been gone, Thomas thought, as he got in position to continue his workout.

"Jario is right for once," Baxter said. "You have greatly improved."

"It felt different this time," Thomas replied. "My blade seemed to move on its own. I didn't have to think about each stroke."

"I could feel your responses to my blade," Baxter said, as he clapped Thomas on the shoulder. "You will have my place in the army before you know it. Now get out of here before I run you through with my blade."

Baxter felt Thomas grip his arm. Seeing the sincerity in Thomas' eyes, Baxter realized they had become good friends. They would stand with each other and defend each other until they were taken from the earth. Feeling the moment was getting to thick with emotion, Baxter kicked Thomas' legs out from under him. Laughing, the two men dropped their blades and began to wrestle on the floor.

After his exercise session with Baxter was over, he headed for his chamber with the thought of a much needed bath and clean clothes. He didn't want to offend Lara with his ripe odor and definitely wanted another chance to kiss her sweet lips. Entering his chamber, he noticed McDuff was just getting ready to leave.

"I filled your tub," responded McDuff. "I knew you would want to clean up after your session in the exercise room."

Thomas looked at McDuff wondering how he knew he would be coming to the room.

"I can read thoughts, sir," responded McDuff, after hearing his question in his mind. "Your fresh clothes are on the bed." He bid Thomas good evening and left the chamber closing the door behind him.

After cleaning up, Thomas made his way back to Tate's room. Lara sat quietly on the cot as Tate slept on the feather mattress across the room. She stood as he entered the room and took his hands leading him to the cot.

"Tate is doing so much better," Lara said, as she inhaled his fresh clean scent. "It won't be long before the council can ask their questions, and we can charge Jario and Magna with their crimes."

Thomas grasped her hand tightly feeling the sensation travelling up his arm and shoulders. He leaned toward her touching her lips softly with the pad of his thumb.

"I have missed you," he whispered and then gently kissed her lips. He wrapped his arms around her and felt her place her head against his shoulder. Kissing the top of her head, he felt heat race through his body. Pulling away slightly, he helped her sit and then sat down beside her.

"I saw Jario in the exercise room tonight," replied Thomas. "It appears that he hasn't missed me since he has been away from the castle. He said that he has been protecting the village and watching a new ship that has arrived in the harbor."

Lara rolled her eyes doubting that there was any truth to Jario's explanation. "The longer we can keep Tate a secret, the better," said Lara.

Nodding in agreement, Thomas put his arm around Lara as they leaned back against the soft pillows of his cot. Lara felt the warm sensation running through her body and enjoyed the security it gave her. She had never felt anything like this before and was anxious for the time they could be alone together. They sat holding each other in silence, and for now, it was enough. Lara could feel Thomas' fingers making circles on her arm. His fingers began to slow, and Lara realized Thomas was beginning to drift off to sleep. Smiling, Lara snuggled closer to Thomas. She heard him begin to softly snore, and Lara closed her eyes thinking of what their life would be like with him as her mate.

Hours later, Tate slowly woke and sat up putting his feet upon the stone floor. He looked around the room seeing Thomas and Lara across from him sitting on the cot sleeping. Thomas had his arm around her, and she had her hand placed on his chest.

"Hey, you lovebirds," Tate shouted. "I'm hungry. When is my dinner coming?"

Startled, Thomas sat up quickly forgetting Lara was snuggled against him. Lara felt his abrupt movement and opened her eyes. Seeing Tate was awake, she felt embarrassed to have been found sleeping next to Thomas. To avoid his eyes, she looked down at her skirt and began to smooth the folds from the fabric. Raising her eyes to Tate, she could see his broad smile and returned one of her own.

"We were just resting," Thomas replied and stood offering his hand to Lara. As she stood, she approached Tate and looked at him carefully. His eyes were no longer red but a bright blue rimmed in black.

"I think it is time to talk. You need to tell us the complete story of how Magna found you and what you heard while you were held in the dungeon," Lara said, as she motioned for Tate to sit at the table.

Tate joined them at the table and prepared to tell his story from the very beginning.

"I spotted Magna standing on the dock when we all left the ship after it had docked in the harbor. She seemed to enjoy the whistles from the crew as we made our way to the old tavern. We were all in need of the taste of ale and to have a little fun with the ladies. Magna followed us into the tavern and approached our table wanting to join us. The men all nodded eagerly, and she sat down next to me. I lost count of the number of ales we consumed, but she kept them coming until I apparently passed out. When I woke, I was chained in a dirty damp cell. There was a young woman named Gavenia beside me. She was kept naked and had bite marks all over her body. Magna would leave us for days without food, water or a way to clean ourselves. When she would return, she would bring raw meat that was full of maggots, but we would eat it because we were so hungry. Magna said she liked to play with us, and the way she played was to torture us. Torture excited her. She clawed at our bodies and made them bleed. She made us lick each other's blood. It was so disgusting. It caused us to vomit. She laughed as she made me hold Gavenia while she abused her body with knives. I was unable to do anything to stop it," cried Tate holding his hands over his face to hide the tears.

"It was compulsion, Tate," replied Lara. "You wouldn't have been able to stop her and would have done anything she told you to do. It isn't your fault."

Tate nodded and continued his story. "I saw Jario one night after Magna had abused me, and I must have passed out from the pain. Waking from my sleep, I saw Jario chained to the cell wall. I thought that she had taken another man prisoner, but I soon found out that Jario was her friend and a willing participant. He took the clawing, biting and any other torture she had to offer until he could stand no more. She carried his naked body to her bed and tenderly cleaned him. She spoke softly to him like a lover would speak. Once his body was clean, she cleaned or own. She put her naked body next to his, and he put his arm around her. They slept and when they woke, the bloody marks and all the injuries on Jario's body were gone. They had just vanished. This is when I heard them talk about kidnapping Lara and making Lara and Jario mates," said Tate, as he watched for a reaction from Thomas.

"After Magna and Jario left, she returned alone. She saw that I was awake, and she told me it was time for me to turn. She tore what was left of my tunic off of my body, grabbed my shoulders and sank her fangs into my neck. The pain was terrible every time she drank my blood, but this time, the pain slowly went away until everything was dark. I could only taste a harsh thick liquid within my mouth. When I opened my eyes, she was gone. My throat burned as if it was on fire. She had moved Gavenia to another cell to keep her from me. Gavenia cried when she saw me wake up. She saw my red eyes and screamed before she fell to the stone floor. I stood and threw myself at the cell bars because of the pain, and suddenly, I realized I was on the other side of the cell. Escape was my only thought. I ran and ran until I was clear of the place that imprisoned me. I know that I killed people. I killed anything I could for the blood. I am so sorry for the killing," he said, as he lowered his eyes and shook his head.

"One evening Jario found me in the forest. Seeing him made me shudder. As I was about to run, Magna appeared and took me back to the cell. She must have thought she left the cell door open or unlocked. Magna didn't seem to know that I could walk through walls. As soon as she left, I left again. I now know that it was you, Thomas, that found me on the ship. I was going to hide there in hopes that the ship would sail, and I would never see Magna or Jario again. You found me again the day I hunted the large buck for a meal. The rest you know," he said, as he looked at Thomas finding understanding in his face.

"I am so sorry that those horrific things happened to you," sighed Lara. "They will never happen again. Since you have released the madness from your mind and are no longer seized by its darkness, you need not be held within this chamber." Hearing a sigh of relief, Lara covered his hands with her own. He was tempted to pull them away, but he needed her comforting touch. "If you believe that you are strong enough, I will bring the council to this chamber. They will want to hear your story. Before I send for the council, I need to release your restraints." She took a key from her pocket and lifted Tate's hand in hers. Tate watched as she unlocked each of the cuffs, and they fell from his wrists.

"Thank you Lady Lara, please bring the council to me. It is time for me to tell them of the horrors I have suffered and of my many crimes. If you and Thomas will stay by my side, I feel I am ready to tell my story," he replied, with another deep sigh. "They need to know what happened in that dungeon. They need to stop them from torturing anyone else."

Chapter 12

Jario left the castle at an all-out run toward the village tavern. He had been avoiding Thomas since he had seen him with Lara at the stables. Seeing Thomas, today, made him furious and anxious to take her from him. It was clear that he would never get her to come to him willingly, and the only way to get her for himself was to kidnap her. He hated to admit it, but Magna was right. Once they were mated, he would take command of the castle. He had to start organizing his own army to be prepared to take over Evergreen. He needed the help of Gusty and Buck.

He flung the door of the tavern open looking for his friends. They sat at their usual table with hands around mugs of ale. Walking over to the table he smacked Gusty on the back of the head.

"Is this all you ever do?" Jario asked, as he pulled over a stool and sat down. Gusty scowled back at Jario and slugged him in the shoulder. Seeing a stranger from the corner of his eye, he asked Buck, "Who is the man over in the corner?" They turned their heads and looked at the man sitting alone in the corner of the tavern.

"We have seen him several times here in the village and down at the docks, over the past year or two," replied Buck. "We know he is a vampire, but he keeps to himself and doesn't appear to have friends here in the village. We have never seen him bother anyone."

Jario stood up and made his way over to the stranger. "I have not seen you here or in the village," Jario said, as he stood with authority. The man tilted his head up slightly to look up at the man standing before him.

"I am called Balgair, and I visit the village from time to time. The big ships bring me," he said, in a strong accent Jario had never heard. "I come to see the old woman, Velsa. Do you know her?"

Surprised that he had never seen him before, he paused thinking of what kind of trouble he and Velsa would be conjuring.

"I do," Jario answered, with a cautious smile and sat down to join Balgair at the table. "The witch has made many bargains with me,"

Jario added to reflect that they also had a friendship.

Balgair acknowledged the fact that she was known to him as a witch by his grin. "I do favors for her too, when she needs certain supplies," he responded. "The payments are good, and the items she requires are easily obtained."

Thinking about his relationship with Velsa and knowing the kinds of favors she bargains for, he thought Balgair might take on a favor of his choosing. "I might have a favor you could do for me. What is your required payment?" Jario anxiously asked.

Balgair scratched his chin with his long fingernails. "It would mean giving up one of your powers to me," he smiled, looking at Jario with a raised eyebrow wondering if he would go that far.

Jario looked shocked. He had never heard of any vampire that was able to take another vampire's powers.

Could he really have enough power to take his gifted powers, he thought?

"Just one would do," Balgair added. "I'll take your power of smoke."

Jario looked surprised and wondered how he knew what powers he had been gifted and asked, "How do you know of my power of smoke?"

"It is easy when you can read powers like I can," he offered, after hearing Jario's thoughts before Jario asked his question.

"I must think on this," responded Jario. "Will you be in the village long?"

Balgair smiled knowing he would be doing a favor for Jario in the near future and retrieving his power of smoke for payment. "I will be here five more nights and then will leave when the ship leaves the harbor," he replied. "Come to this tavern when you are ready, and I will be here waiting for you. I will know when you are ready."

Jario left the tavern in a rush to see Magna. "Could this really be happening?" Jario said, into the wind. He would have help kidnapping Lady Lara and taking her to the Canyon of Obscurity. He would finally have her.

* * *

Entering the dungeon, he found Magna leaning over the young woman with her fangs in her thigh. Jario stepped into the cell and grabbed her by her hair.

"We have to talk," he said sternly. She pulled from his grasp and wiped her mouth with the back of her hand, as she followed Jario over to the velvet bench at the foot of the bed.

"Why Jario, are you back to play so soon?" Magna sneered happily as her fingers began to unlace her corset.

He shook his head in disgust as he grabbed her hand stopping her from freeing her breasts from her corset. Letting go of her hand, he stepped back and peered over her shoulder looking for the young man that had been sharing the cell.

"I spoke with a vampire at the tavern this evening. He says that he knows Velsa. He told me he has done favors for her, and he is willing to do me a favor. If he does, he requires payment of one of my powers. Have you heard of any vampire that can take a gifted power?" he asked, as he gripped her hands to keep her focused.

"What could you possibly want so badly that you would be willing to give away your power?" she replied. "Wait... You are going to do it. You want his help kidnapping my sister, Lara. Is she really worth losing a power?"

Jario stood and paced back and forth in front of Magna running his hands through his hair in frustration. Losing one of his powers in exchange for the chance to rule Evergreen Castle would be worth it and glorious. There was certainly a risk involved since the man was a stranger in the village, and he needed to be very cautious. Even though he knew Velsa, it didn't make him trustworthy. He decided he needed to make a visit to Velsa's cottage.

* * *

The cottage sat deep in the woods that surrounded the Black Thistle Castle. If Velsa didn't want to be disturbed, she would simply hide her dwelling from view with one of her many spells. He had been searching for hours and feared the sun would start to make its appearance before he could find it. Almost giving up, he turned around to leave and spotted a slight glow within the trees, off in the distance. Heading toward the light, he could see the cottage hidden among a thick patch of trees. Reaching his destination, he knocked on the wooden door and waited. There was no response. He noticed a shadow move across the dirty window and knew she was inside.

"Velsa, it is Jario," he shouted. "I have come to talk to you about a bargain. Open the door."

The door creaked as it opened, and he stepped inside. He could not stand fully due to the ceiling covered in rows and rows of drying herbs. He looked around and saw her sitting by the fire.

"Come in kind sir," she croaked, as she spoke giving the impression that something may have been lodged in her throat. She coughed and spit into the fire as she watched the flames explode with dark purple sparks. "You desire a bargain with me?"

He prudently approached the old witch and sat upon a small milking stool near her chair. Balancing his large frame upon the wobbly stool, he tried to draw her attention away from a spider that crawled across her black leather boot. He watched her pick it up between her fingers and drop it into a wooden bowl. Before it could crawl out, she snapped her fingers and a wooden plate moved over the bowl sealing it inside.

Clearing his throat, Jario tried to gain her attention before he spoke. "There is a man, Balgair, in the village that I wish to ask a favor," he said, watching her eyes for recognition. "He is to take someone to the Canyon of Obscurity for me. In return, he wants my gifted power of smoke in payment."

The witch looked at him with a questioned look. "Why do you come here seeking a bargain? It appears the bargain is with the vampire called Balgair," she replied.

"Yes, this bargain will be with him," replied Jario, as he fidgeted on the stool. "I want to know if he can be trusted. Will he follow through on the bargain or just simply take my power and leave?" Jario looked at Velsa with concern and worry in his eyes.

"I have had many a favor performed by the vampire called Balgair. He has not betrayed me," she responded.

Jario felt satisfied after hearing her response, but he was still anxious to make a bargain with her. "Knowing he is trustworthy, I wish to make a bargain with you. I am going to the Canyon of Obscurity and want to keep my remaining powers when I enter it. Can you give me a potion or perform a spell that will allow me this protection?" Jario asked, knowing it would cost him.

"That is a simple request, but the payment will be more difficult and one that cannot be denied. I ask for three favors of my choosing. These favors will be paid at the time of my choosing," she replied. "Do you agree with this payment?"

He nodded and felt a mix of relief and concern as his shoulders relaxed. He could worry about the required payment later.

Velsa stood and began to take items from the ceiling and dig her fingers into several jars on the table pulling out what looked like moldy salve. Catching a small mouse that ran across the table, she crushed it in her hand and threw it into a wooden bowl along with the other items she had collected. She began to chant. She swayed from side to side and her hair stood straight up to the ceiling mingling with the harvested herbs. The smell that came from the bowl was revolting and small sparks flew from the rim. When her chanting stopped, she poured the foul liquid into a small bottle with a gold cap. Seeing the liquid had burned a hole in the bottom of the bowl, she threw the bowl into the fire. It exploded and made sounds like screeching birds. She handed the small bottle to Jario.

If it burned a hole in the bowl, I wonder what it would do to me, Jario thought, as he took the bottle from her outstretched hand.

"Drink this just before you step into the canyon. It will only last five days. If you are still within the canyon beyond five days, you will lose your powers permanently. Whatever evil you have planned will have ramifications on all who dwell on this land. Beware the revenge this may cause upon you," she warned, staring deeply into his eyes. "I know of what I speak. I have suffered from my own desires."

"I will heed your warnings," Jario responded. Putting the bottle in the pocket of his jacket, he bowed slightly to the witch and left the cottage.

Wondering if he had made a mistake, he turned to look back at the cottage to find it gone.

Chapter 13

The council met with Tate and had all the information they needed to charge Jario and Magna with feeding from and torturing a human, in addition to, plotting to kidnap Lady Lara. They planned to arrest him in the exercise room upon his return. The army would be near and make capturing Jario much easier.

Thomas led his brother down to the exercise room. There he would start his training with Baxter. Entering the large room, Tate could see several men brandishing swords and others fighting in hand to hand combat. He could tell that there were both vampires and humans in the room, as well as, men and women. Baxter looked up to see Thomas with his brother. He dropped his quiver of arrows to the stone floor and ran over to officially meet Tate. Baxter offered his hand to Tate and greeted him with a smile.

"Welcome to the army," he said, as he slapped Tate on the shoulder. "We have looked forward to meeting you and are looking forward to you teaching us the skills you learned manning the big ships. In return, we'll teach you how to knock your brother on his ass." Baxter laughed and looked at Thomas for a reaction.

Thomas laughed and said, "Let's get to work."

Thomas and Tate had only been working on the mats for a few minutes when Preston came running into the room shouting," Jario has been spotted by the lookout. He is coming this way. Men prepare to take him down when he has made his way to the center of the room. Tate, I want you to go to the side room. I don't want Jario to see you until it is too late. He'll know that he has been caught if he sees you, and he'll try to make his escape."

Tate ran to the side room and closed the door. Everyone else continued to spar and work about the room as if nothing was wrong.

Jario entered the room and nodded when Baxter looked up.

"Just the vampire I wanted to see," shouted Baxter.

Jario saw Preston in the corner of the room talking to some of the other men and knew that he couldn't ignore Baxter without drawing attention to himself. Walking over to Baxter he wondered what stupid assignment he had waiting for him. It seemed like he always got the worst of the assignments. He hated that Baxter was human and giving him orders. Once he was in charge of this place, humans would be reduced to supplying the daily nourishment, not leading the castle army.

"What can I do for you?" asked Jario.

"Lady Lara has another new vampire to train. Our Lady thought you would be the perfect vampire to get him started," replied Baxter with a grin.

He hated that grin. "When will he be released for me to start?" asked Jario, looking around to see if he might already be here.

"He is in the side room getting changed and should be out shortly. Besides, you have nothing better to do this evening, right?" joked Baxter.

The door to the side room opened. As Tate walked out of the room, he was pulling a tunic over his head. Having trouble getting his arm in the sleeve, the awkward motion kept his face covered a little longer. This gave him a chance to get further into the room without Jario recognizing him. Jario looked at the vampire and rolled his eyes.

"You want me to teach him to fight. I think I will ask McDuff to teach him how to dress himself first," he joked, as he looked at Baxter rolling his eyes in disgust.

Looking back over at the vampire, Tate now stood with his tunic in place. It took a moment, but Jario finally recognized the vampire as the man Magna had held in the Black Thistle Castle dungeon.

Several of the men in the room moved to block the doorways. Preston stepped forward and shouted, "Jario, you are under arrest for the acts of torture upon humans and the plot to kidnap our Lady Lara. Guards take him to the dungeon."

Jario stood in complete shock. Knowing the penalty for treason, he needed to get away fast, before they took his head. He couldn't believe that this vampire had survived Magna's clutches or knew about the plot he and Magna had discussed. He quickly summoned his haze and was now invisible to the men coming toward him. Pushing his smoke in a thick and suffocating layer, it slowed the humans as they coughed and gagged trying to breathe. Jario ran from the room knocking unsuspecting men out of the way. Once outside the door, he sped away with lightning speed and knew that he had to warn Magna.

* * *

Jario had spent most of the evening with Magna trying to come up with a plan to remove Lara from the castle. Now that Evergreen knew of his plot, he was sure they had enlisted the witch, Meadow, to offer some kind of protection spell.

She wouldn't be bound to the castle, he thought, as he stood and looked at Magna, or she would then be a prisoner in her own castle.

"Meadow must have cast a spell to protect her from us," Jario said out loud, as he frantically paced Magna's chamber. His words startled Magna, and she glared at him turning to walk back to the young woman in the cell. "Can you forget your blood lust for one moment and help me figure out what to do? The army will be coming for us," he shouted. "Your little pet, the one you let slip from his cell, will lead them right to us."

Ignoring Jario, she bent down and picked up the young woman looking at her naked body. Seeing the numerous bite marks still covered with freshly clotted blood, she dropped the woman to floor and walked back to Jario licking the blood from her fingers.

"I need a new pet. Help me find a new pet," she said, as she looked directly into his eyes and pouted. "This one is almost dead."

"I have to find Balgair," he spoke out load.

Thinking to himself, he may just be the vampire that could help him.

"Magna, go to Velsa and have her shield the castle," ordered Jario. "Do it now! She will want to bargain. Give her what she asks."

He dashed through the doorway leaving Magna frustrated as she bent to pull on her boots and make a visit to Velsa's cottage.

* * *

Jario entered the tavern as his eyes darted around the room looking for Balgair. Just as he had said, he was sitting at the same table in the back of the room. Walking anxiously across the room and pulling a stool over to the table to sit across from him, he watched Balgair lift his head and give him a wicked smile.

"You have decided to give me your smoke," he said, already knowing of his decision.

"Yes," Jario replied. "I ask for a favor. In return, I will give you my power of smoke."

Balgair sniffed the air and frowned at Jario. "I smell it on you. You have used it recently," he said, as he looked suspiciously at Jario.

"I was in need of a quick escape and used it to halt some humans that were after me," he replied, with a half-truth, as he looked at Balgair hoping he wouldn't ask any more questions.

"Let us go outside where it is more private. There, you can properly request a favor of me," Balgair replied, as he stood and headed for the tavern door. Jario followed him quickly through the door and moved to the side of the tavern out of the light of the burning lantern and into the shadows.

"I ask that you take Lady Lara from Evergreen Castle to the Canyon of Obscurity," whispered Jario.

Balgair knew he would be able to acquire the lady for him but cross into the Canyon of Obscurity was beyond his willingness. "I agree to acquire Lady Lara for you, but I will only bring her to the border of the canyon. I will not cross it, and I believe you know why," responded Balgair with a stern look.

"I understand," Jario replied, feeling his hands shake in anticipation of having her within his grasp.

"Tomorrow evening, meet me at the border, and I will hand you your lady," Balgair said, as the favor was agreed.

"Now stand still, if you can, while I remove your smoke to fulfill your payment," Balgair requested, as he brought his hands to Jario's chest.

Jario felt a deep burning sensation and then he dropped to his knees in horrible pain. His chest began to glow deep red. He watched as a black vapor began to leave his body and swirl in the air, searching for freedom. Balgair began to inhale through is mouth making a strangled shrieking sound. The black vapor fought Balgair at first, but then it slowly disappeared into his mouth as he swallowed and licked his thin lips. Jario blinked in disbelief. Still kneeling on the ground, he watched Balgair turn and walk from the tavern and disappear into the darkness.

"It is going to work," Jario spoke, loudly to himself. "It has to work."

Chapter 14

After the smoke cleared from the room and it was determined Jario had escaped, Preston barked orders to organize a search party. Knowing the powers that Jario had been gifted made the possibility of finding him quickly or arresting him out in the open unlikely. He was just too powerful. This would not deter them from trying to capture him. The act of treason meant that they would never stop until he was arrested.

Lara heard the yelling and smelled the smoke. She came running to see if they had captured Jario.

"My Lady, he got away," Preston said, as he knelt in apology.

"It is not your fault. Jario is sly and will use every trick in the book to his advantage," Lara replied, as she knelt down taking Preston's hands and lifting them to make him stand. "He won't be coming back here. Now that he knows what we know of him, he will have to find sanctuary someplace else."

Tate approached Lara. "I believe I might know where you can find Magna and possibly Jario, as well. Magna had me held in the dungeon. I heard her call it the Black Thistle Castle. I am not sure, but I believe that she might still be there."

Lara looked back at her Army Commander. "Preston, send Tate and some of your men to the Black Thistle Castle and look for Magna," Lara ordered. "Before they leave, take Tate to the Room of Powers. We need to know what additional powers we have available for the fight."

"Yes, My Lady," replied Preston, as he left quickly with Tate on his heels.

* * *

Preston pulled a key from his leather pouch and unlocked the heavy door. Tate could hear the same sounds that Thomas had described.

"This is the Room of Powers," Preston explained. "It contains all the powers that could be gifted to a vampire. We know that you can walk through walls and can leap a great distance. We are here to find out what other powers have been gifted to you. Do not be afraid, the sound you hear are from the Wispets that protect the Room of Powers. They take care of the powers and make sure they stay strong. They are not prisoners here in this room and can leave through a portal inside the chamber. They come and go, but are always present when the Wispet Queen performs the Gifting Ceremony."

Preston opened the door and held it open for Tate to enter. Seeing the stone pillar that Thomas had described, Tate stepped forward looking about the room and finally letting his eyes rest upon the inscription on the pillar. A sudden glow appeared above the pillar. He watched as a tiny woman appeared wearing a gown of white. The layers of shimmery fabric were embellished with green and lavender threads. A crown rested above her eyes and her hair was the palest shade of lavender he had ever seen.

"Step forward Tate," she spoke softly. "Step forward and place your hands upon the pillar."

Tate stepped forward and placed his hands upon the flat surface of the pillar. He could feel the indentations of the carved inscription beneath his fingers. As he did, the globes about the room began to brighten. Five globes drifted down to the pillar and nestled themselves against each other.

He watched as the Wispet Queen touched the first clear globe. It turned dark blue, and a word in a language he could not read appeared above the surface of the pillar. "Walk through Walls," she said, as the word disappeared and the globe's light faded. As she touched the next globe, it began to brighten to the color of the evergreens he loved so much. "Compulsion," she announced, as he watched the globe fade like the first. Touching the next globe, it began to brighten. It became too bright and made him close his eyes. "Walk in Daylight," she said, as he felt the air sizzle before the light dimmed, and he could finally open his eyes. Tapping the next globe lightly, it changed quickly into a bright orange. He could feel the heat coming from the globe and feared it would burn his hands. "Hands of Fire," she said, as she waved her hand over the globe, and it instantly cooled and faded. She touched the last globe, and he watched it turn purple and pulse with light. "Great Leaping," she said, as the globe tried to move off the pillar. The Wispet Queen smiled and touched it lightly, making it sit perfectly still. "These five gifts have been given," declared the Wispet Queen. She looked directly into Tate's eyes. Seeing him bow his head in appreciation, she smiled and offered her final words, "Use them well." The Wispet Queen faded from view. Tate could hear the chatter and laughter of tiny voices for a moment and then it was quiet, returning the room to dim candlelight. The globes began to float into the air and swirl about Tate's head, making a strange buzzing sound. One by one, they returned to their place upon the shelves.

"We are finished here," spoke Preston. "We need to head back to the group and inform My Lady of what you have been gifted. It is a shame you will not be able to practice any of these gifts before you set out on the search."

* * *

As they entered the room, several groups of humans and vampires were readying themselves to leave the castle to search for Magna and Jario. Thomas saw Preston and Tate enter the room and ran to meet his brother.

"Brother, what were you gifted," he asked, anxious to hear of his gifts.

"I received five gifts," replied Tate. "Walk through Walls, Compulsion, Walk in Daylight, Hands of Fire and Great Leaping were all gifted to me."

Thomas slapped his brother on the back as he asked, "Did you leave any for anyone else?"

Everyone laughed for a moment. It was probably more from nervous energy than the look on Tate's face as it reddened.

Preston shouted, "Command One, take Tate and head for the Black Thistle Castle. Two, search the forest surrounding it. Three, set up surveillance at the Canyon of Obscurity. He may try to escape through the canyon to Whistler River and beyond. Four, you will guard Evergreen Castle and My Lady. Any questions?" The silence was deafening.

"With Honor," Preston shouted. "With Honor," the army shouted in reply and left running to their assignments.

Lara stood watching the army leave the castle. "I should be going with them to hunt down Jario and my sister," she angrily shouted. "Not be kept here in a box. I will not break. I can fight and should be searching with my army."

Thomas stepped up behind her and put his hand gently at her back.

"Don't worry My Lady," said Preston. "They will find them. Besides, Evergreen needs you here. Your people cannot afford to lose you. We will protect you with our lives."

She returned a smile to Preston appreciating his need to protect her, but also felt helpless. She was Evergreen's Mistress and needed to be protected for the sake of her people. However, she was also a warrior and could fight alongside her army, if allowed to do so.

"Let me take you back to your chamber?" Thomas asked.

Lara nodded her head knowing there wasn't anything more that she could do, and they turned to leave for her chamber. Elda followed closely behind them.

As they reached her chamber door, Thomas opened the door slowly to let Lara pass through into her chamber and then stepped back to leave.

"Please don't go," pleaded Lara. "Stay and keep me company this evening. I will spend my time worrying for the others, if I am left alone."

Thomas stepped into the chamber. He glanced at Elda as she took up her post by the chamber door. He closed the door sliding the bolt. Lara stood waiting for him to come to her. As she closed her eyes, she could hear each step he took across the stone floor. When she could feel him in front of her, she lifted her arms placing them around his waist and her face against his chest.

"You give me so much comfort," she sighed softly. "It has given me so much happiness having you here at the castle."

"I hope that once Magna and Jario are caught, I can make you happier still," Thomas said, as he ran his fingers in soft circles against her back.

They sat quietly beside the fire holding one another watching the fire slowly reduce to embers. Thomas kissed her lips lightly, savoring the feel of her body resting against his own. He knew that he wanted Lara for his own and for all eternity. He felt that she cared for him, but she was royalty and far above his station.

Feeling her fingers against his skin beneath his tunic, he struggled to control his arousal. He closed his eyes and reveled in the heat of her touch. He knew that this was not the time to lose control of his desires. Pulling her hand from his body, he kissed her finger tips and held them against his chest.

"I am falling in love with you," he whispered in her ear. Inhaling her sweet scent, he kissed her forehead. "I could easily take you. I feel your desire for me, but it is not the time to follow our desires."

"I have fallen in love with you," she responded, as she looked into his eyes. "I will wait as you ask. I will be yours when the time is right."

Thomas felt his body shudder after hearing her words. He kissed her forehead and tried to calm his arousal.

"We shall speak more of love once Jario and your sister are captured," he said. "Now is the time for level heads and presently you are driving me to the point where I have no control over mine."

Lara smiled and snuggled closer to him. Opening the neck of his tunic, her fingers brushed the hairs on his chest. Looking up to find his silver-gray eyes, she felt him capture her mouth with his, and let the heat of desire rush through her body. His kiss was heavenly and all that she would enjoy until the time was right for them to be together.

Once the darkness was gone and morning began to paint bright spots of light upon the stone floor, Thomas closed the shutters and drapes.

I have seen these drapes before, he thought, remembering his first vision.

A soft tap upon the door was heard by Thomas. He unlocked the door cautiously and saw Flora waiting to enter.

"I am here to ready My Lady for bed," she said to Thomas wondering why he was in her chamber.

"Come in. I was just taking my leave," he said, as he turned to look at Lara sitting by the fire. "I will be back this evening. If you feel up to it, we can go check on Arrow. It would be good to see him and take your mind off things."

"Thomas, that would be wonderful," replied Lara, as she noticed Flora enter the room.

Thomas left the chamber anxious to get back to the Command Center. He passed Elda and turned to ask if she needed anything. Elda shook her head, and Thomas left with haste back to the Command Center.

* * *

Jario sat in the dark behind the rocks that rimmed the Canyon of Obscurity. Spending the whole day hidden in the base of a hollowed out tree in the forest, he smelled of decomposed leaves and had spider webs covering his clothes and hair. It was disgusting to have to hide like an animal, but it would be worth all of it once he could get his hands on Lara. The army of humans had made their way into the forest during the daylight hours with the aid of horses, and he had heard them searching for him. His haze had been the only thing that had saved him. Now that his smoke was gone, he only had the haze, compulsion, and stone to protect him.

He wondered who had caught the new vampire and where they had found him. It was obvious that he had told them everything he had heard, everything while he was held in Magna's dungeon cell. He knew he had spent too much time away from the castle, but he couldn't be with Magna and at Evergreen Castle at the same time. He felt for his pouch. It was still secure about his waist. Losing the potion would be the ruin of all he planned.

Chapter 15

Thomas approached Lara's chamber door. Elda still stood on guard at her door. She was a faithful servant to Lady Lara and the castle.

"Have you fed or slept since I left you this morning?" Thomas asked, with concern in his voice.

"Yes, Charlotte brought me a meal. I don't require sleep. It was one of my gifts," she replied, as she grinned at him.

He started to knock on her door, but it opened and Lara greeted him with a smile. "Good evening," she spoke, trying to hide the worry that she felt.

"Shall we visit the new colt and his mother?" he replied. Her eyes brightened as she stepped toward Thomas. Elda closed the door and stood ready to follow them to the stables.

Lara could hear the young colt thrashing about the stall. As she peered over the gate into the stall, she could see the young black colt thrash about the feet of his mother. Mona nudged him gently with her nose, and he stood for a moment watching Lara. Then seeming uninterested with his visitors, he nuzzled under his mother for his evening meal.

"He is so beautiful and has grown so much since my last visit," Lara spoke softly, as she entered the stall and put her hands gently upon Mona's nose. She leaned in and kissed her nose and whispered so only Mona could hear, "I love you."

The stall was becoming too small for the mare and her colt, and she knew she should speak to Tolin about moving them to a larger one. Thomas stood outside the stall leaning on the gate enjoying the view of Lara as she lovingly stroked Mona's head and whispered sweet words to her.

Seeing the young colt starting to grow weary, Lara kissed Mona one last time and opened the gate to leave the stall. Lara moved toward the open end of the stables and looked up at the sky.

"Have you ever seen so many beautiful stars?" Lara asked Thomas.

He stepped forward and placed his hand against her back. "It is a nice night for a walk," he replied. "The moon is out in its full glory, lighting the grounds."

He looked at Elda to see if she thought it would be safe. Elda stepped forward just beyond Lady Lara and Thomas to scan the surrounding area. Finding it clear, she turned and stepped aside nodding and letting Thomas and Lady Lara pass her.

They walked arm in arm for just a few yards. Lara stopped and looked up into the night sky. Thomas followed her gaze, and they both spotted a shooting star.

"Quick," Lara said, grabbing Thomas' hand. "Make a wish."

They both closed their eyes and made a wish. Lara read Thomas' thoughts and was delighted to know what he wished. She had wished the same thing, a life together for all eternity.

The night was cool and a breeze made Lara shiver. When she felt a much colder breeze brush against her back she gasped. Thomas had felt the cold breeze too. He turned to place his arm around Lara and saw Elda standing frozen in place with a look of fright upon her face. Thomas moved Lara behind his back and pulled his dagger from his boot.

"I see nothing around us," he said, to Lara as he felt behind his back for her hand. He backed up further wanting Lara to touch him to let him know that she was there. "Lara?" he said, with panic in his voice.

Hearing nothing, he turned to see a tall sliver of a man holding Lara by his side. Her eyes were closed, as if sleeping.

"I am very sorry. It is just a favor," the man said. He vanished leaving a stream of silver mist twirling where they had stood.

Thomas fell to his knees screaming, "No! He has taken her!"

* * *

Without warning, a silver mist rose from the ground as Balgair and Lady Lara appeared at the rim of the Canyon. Seeing them, Jario jumped from the rocks looking about waiting for the army to grab them.

"Your favor is complete," said Balgair.

He placed her hand in Jario's and stepped back away from them, not trusting how close they were to the edge of the canyon. Jario seized her hand tightly as he grappled with the pouch at his waist. Finally retrieving the bottle with one hand, he dislodged the top with his thumb and brought the bottle to his mouth. He paused for a moment to give a nod to Balgair. Placing the bottle on his lips, he tipped it up letting the potion pour into his mouth. Expecting something painful to happen, he was surprised when he felt nothing. He would curse the witch if she had tricked him. He looked up once more to see Balgair, but he was gone. Feeling as if he were being watched, he pulled Lara tightly against his body, and he put his arms around her waist. Looking over the edge of the canyon, he jumped.

* * *

The darkness along with the wind blowing franticly through the canyon made it difficult to see much beyond Jario's outstretched hand. He normally had excellent vision in the dark, but this darkness was thick and felt heavy. It hung about him like a hooded cloak as he carried her over his shoulder along the edge of the empty stream.

There were rumored to be stone dwellings still within the canyon. Remains of dwellings once used by the Wispets before they were driven from the canyon during the War of the Witches. The canyon had withered once the Wispets left. The streams no longer ran with crystal clear water, and the trees stood twisted and dry without their leaves. The lavender that once made the canyon full of a sweet fragrance were now full of brambles and smelled of decay. Everything that was good about the canyon was gone, including the powers of anyone who entered it.

Jario continued walking through the remains of fallen trees and thick clusters of weeds until he spotted a small stone cottage almost hidden from view. A large tree had fallen and what was left of the branches covered most of the cottage. The panes of the windows were cracked, and the door hung on one broken hinge. Making his way to the doorway, Jario bent down low to enter the cottage. He could barely stand inside without hitting his head upon the rotting beams of the ceiling. Looking about the small room, he saw what appeared to be a cot or small bed in the corner against the wall. Putting Lara down upon the dusty coverlet, he was grateful she still slept and was unable to fight him. He found some rope left hanging upon a rusted spike and began to tie it about her hands tethering it to the wooden frame of the bed. Once he was sure she was secure, he walked about the room laughing. It had been too easy. He had fooled them all.

He stepped outside ready to test his powers. He pulled for his haze and it came quickly. With relief, he picked up a dead tree branch and tightened his hand around it feeling it harden and turn to stone. He still had his powers. Grinning, he strutted back into the cottage.

Finding a chair he thought would hold him, he carefully sat down and leaned back stretching his legs out to wait for her to wake.

Chapter 16

The army of humans and vampires made their way slowly through the Evergreen Forest being careful to watch for any signs of Jario or Magna. Not all of the vampires could walk in the daylight and any plans to arrive at their ordered destinations would have to take that into consideration. Reaching the edge of the forest, it was clear that the vampires would not be able to cross the sprawling meadow that separated the two castles before the sun began to rise. Even with Tate's power of leaping, he would not be able to assist every vampire across quickly enough. It was determined the humans and those vampires that could walk in daylight would continue the journey across the meadow. This would leave the remaining vampires in the shelter of the forest until darkness once again was upon them. This cut the three commands down dramatically in size and strength. Along with numbers, the powers that would have been available were also lost.

Reaching the thistles that surrounded Black Thistle Castle, the men started to separate into their command units. They shook each other's hands and wished each other good luck. The men looked at the crumbling castle as they passed and were grateful to be heading for the shelter of the forest. They had heard the rumors of death for those that entered its walls and quickened their steps.

Tate, Baxter and two other vampires, Oliver and Will, made their way to a small path that had been worn among the thistles. Will, a fairly new vampire, was tall with long red hair and thinner than anyone in the army. He acquired Beanpole as a nickname when he first joined the army. It wasn't long before he earned everyone's admiration when he became one of the best with the crossbow, and his nickname was forgotten. Oliver was a huge vampire with muscular shoulders and thighs. He was known more for his strong laugh and his love of the ladies, but he had beaten everyone in the army with his dagger skills.

Oliver tried to avoid the thorns of the thistles, but he soon had deep gashes in his flesh where the thistles snagged his breeches as he walked toward the castle. Seeing the blood run down his legs and onto the path, he noticed the thistles seemed to move about reaching toward him.

"I think we have a problem. These damn thistles are moving," shouted Oliver to the other men. "They are reaching for my blood." He swung his sword and watched as they moved to avoid his blade. The thistles began to circle around Oliver preventing him from moving.

Tate and Will turned and looked at Oliver, as more and more thistles moved in his direction. Tate moved quickly toward Oliver and reached for his arm. Oliver grabbed hold of Tate. He leaped from the spot and landed just next to the drawbridge that was lowered over the black churning mud that filled the moat. Leaping back to Baxter and Will, he grabbed them both and landed next to Oliver as he was examining the damage the thistles had made to his legs.

"Those critters are alive," Baxter said, as he looked at Oliver's bleeding legs that had started to heal. "That gift of yours saved us. They would have torn us to shreds for our blood."

Looking out over the field of thistles surrounding them, Tate saw them reaching for the blood Oliver had left upon the ground. They appeared to fight with each other for the few drops of blood he had left behind.

"I should have remembered what those things can do," said Tate looking somewhat ashamed. "They attacked me when I escaped from this castle. I'm sorry Oliver."

Oliver slapped Tate on the shoulder and responded, "A few blood sucking weeds are the least of our worries. Let's get inside this pile of stones and see what we can find."

Carefully stepping across the rotten planks of the drawbridge that hung precariously over the moat, the men kept their swords ready. Baxter watched the mud in the moat come alive as it crept closer to the bridge. They all moved more quickly trying to avoid the holes in the rotted planks and the mud that franticly reached for their boots.

"This place is bewitched," whispered Baxter, as he stabbed at the mud that had made its way onto the bridge. He then shook the mud from his sword watching it ease itself back into the moat.

Entering the courtyard of the castle, they could hear the haunted sounds in the wind that many built their rumors upon. Stones lay in piles against the collapsing walls. A charred wooden door hung by a twisted piece of metal and moved with each gust of wind. The War of the Witches had demolished the castle, but it had worsened from the weather and neglect.

"Stay here, I am going to head for the dungeon. I can get there through the walls much quicker than all of us taking the hallways. Keep alert, Magna may be in the castle, and she has a great power over men, human and vampire," said Tate, as he handed his sword to Baxter. "I'll be back shortly." Tate walked to the closest wall and stepped directly through the thick stones.

Within the castle walls, he could hear the dripping of water onto the ragged stone floor. He tried to remember the path he had taken when he escaped from the dungeon, but it was all a blur in his mind. He scanned the walls for any clues as he slowly walked the hallways. Seeing the remains of a twisted rope on the floor, he vaguely remembered tripping over it when he escaped the first time. Trusting he was heading in the right direction, he followed the hallway finding a set of stone steps that lead downward. He took the steps as quickly and quietly as he could, being cautious at every step. The further he went, the more light he could see coming from below, making it clear he was going in the right direction. Almost to the bottom of the stairs, he could see burning torches reflecting flashes of light against the wall. He listened for any signs of Magna walking about or the sickening sounds of her feeding. The only sound he could hear was of someone struggling to breathe. Cautiously, he stepped off the last step and onto the dungeon floor. The room was empty except for what looked like a small animal curled up in the corner of a cell. Stepping closer to take a better look, he realized it wasn't an animal at all. It was a woman. Standing next to the cell door, he looked over the woman's body curled in a fetal position. He remembered the young woman that shared a cell with him.

Surely, she couldn't still be alive after all the abuse he had seen her take at the hands of Jario and Magna?

Kneeling by the cell, he softly asked, "Gavenia? Is that you?"

She tried to lift her head, but she was too weak. He passed through the cell bars and bent to turn her face toward him. He pulled back in shock as he barely recognized the young woman. She had cuts and bruises about her face. Her eyes were swollen shut and her red hair had been pulled from her head showing patches of scalp covered in blood.

"I'm here to help you," he whispered in her ear. "I am going to take you from this horrid place and will do my best not to hurt you."

Picking her up as carefully as he could, she moaned as she rested her head against his chest. He didn't know if he could pass through the cell bars with her in his arms, but he had to try. Stepping close to the bars, he took a big step forward and they both passed through to the other side. Slowly he moved toward the steps. Anticipating the arrival of Magna at any time, he swiftly took the stone steps and found his way back to the courtyard where the men waited. Seeing Tate running across the courtyard, the men gathered around him and the battered woman. Seeing she was naked, Will removed his tunic and covered her body.

A vicious scream pierced the air coming from inside the castle. The men knew they had been discovered. Backing toward the main entrance to the courtyard, the men scanned the area for any sign of Magna.

"We need to get Gavenia out of here," shouted Tate.

The men watched as Tate began to cross the wooden drawbridge with her in his arms. Following behind keeping their backs to him, they kept their swords drawn aware that Magna could appear at any moment. Just as they stepped to the ground beyond the drawbridge a glimmer encased the castle.

"A spell has been cast over the castle," yelled Oliver. He could feel the pulsing of the spell as it covered the entire castle. "We made it out, just in time."

As Tate prepared to leap with Gavenia, a red wisp of smoke began to appear in the middle of the bridge. The scent of smoldering coals invaded their nostrils.

"It's Magna," Will shouted, as he bent his knees and readied himself for her attack.

"Baxter, take her," Tate shouted, as he handed Gavenia's limp body to him. "Keep her safe."

Watching the smoke clear, Magna stood feet spread in an arrogant stance. Her eyes blazed red as the air around her snapped and crackled. She pushed a surge of smoldering air in their direction and watched them try to avoid it.

"You have something that belongs to me," Magna hollered at the men, as she licked her lips and flicked her tongue against an extended fang.

"She is no longer yours," Tate shouted, back at Magna as he stood ready for battle. "She belongs to me, now."

Magna's head turned in his direction. Studying him for a moment, a smirk appeared across her face. "Oh! I recognize you now, my little pet. Come back to me, and we can enjoy each other as we did for so many nights." Licking her lips, she took a few steps closer to Tate.

Don't look at her eyes, she has the gift of compulsion," Tate sternly ordered. "Magna, you are to be arrested and returned to the Evergreen Castle for sentencing."

Her laughter filled the air as Magna stepped closer to the men. "Arrest me? I would like to see you try," she sneered and slid her hands down her body seductively. "What makes you think you have enough power to arrest me?"

Tate bravely stepped forward with his sword at ready. Magna flicked her wrist and the sword flew from Tate's hands.

"Your weapons do not scare me. You are but a few weak vampires that have not honed your gifts. You could never take me on your own," she laughed, as she bent down to dust dirt from her boot exposing the fullness of her breasts.

"I have my orders," shouted Tate, as he moved closer to Magna. He could feel the electricity surrounding her body and fear began to creep into his mind.

She glared at him allowing him to move even closer. Once he was within a few feet, she sprang forward and grabbed his arm. He struggled to free himself from her grasp. The more he struggled the tighter she grasped his arm.

"You are coming with me," she laughed and began to build a tendril of red smoke for her escape back into the castle.

He grabbed her arm with his other hand trying to pull his arm free from her grasp. The harder he pulled the more she laughed. The red smoke about them grew larger, and he knew that any second they would be whisked away into the castle. If that happened, he would be lost behind the protection spell.

Remembering his gifts, he looked at his hands. He was able to grab Magna's arm, now, with both hands. He pulled the thought of fire with his mind, and his hands began to burn. In a flash there were flames coming from his hands. Magna's eyes grew wild with fear as she pulled and pulled trying to get her arm away from Tate. Finally she jerked her arm with all her might, leaving the lower part of her arm in Tate's hands. The shocked look upon her face was the last thing the men saw before she vanished. Tate looked at the remains of her arm and hurled it into the moat. The black mud seemed to fight for the privilege of pulling the limb below the surface. As it sank into the mud, red steam hissed and swirled up into the air.

"We have to get Gavenia back to the castle," shouted Baxter feeling her breathing become erratic and hearing her gasp for air.

Tate took Gavenia from his arms and prepared to leap. "I should be able to get her back to the castle quicker than any of you," he responded. "She needs help or she will die." Looking over at Oliver he saw him nod his head, as he helped pull the tunic back up tucking it around her body. "I'll move Gavenia to the open meadow and come back to help you avoid the deadly thistles."

"Oliver, you head back to the castle with Baxter and inform the commander of the spell around the castle. Will, make your way back to the unit and inform them of what happened here. They should move on to help the others search the forest for the traitor and forget the Black Thistle Castle for now. We won't be able to enter the castle and Magna won't be in any condition to bother us for some time." Tate looked at the men to make sure they were all in agreement.

Oliver glared at Baxter as he said, "I'm not walking all the way back to the castle. You'll have to ride back."

Baxter had his usual grin and responded smiling, "Fine with me. Just let me ride on your back because that over the shoulder thing you do, makes my insides ache." Oliver and Baxter playfully jabbed at each other as Will tried to keep from getting knocked into the thistles.

"Will, once I get help for Gavenia, I'll head back to help you search for Jario," he shouted, as he leapt high into the air. Landing within the meadow he placed her gently down among the wildflowers. Standing, he stared at her for a moment feeling warmth leave his chest. Turning back toward the castle, he leapt into the air again to assist the others.

* * *

Lara's eyes fluttered softly as she began to wake from the sleeping spell cast by Balgair. Jario had been daydreaming of power over Evergreen Castle when he saw the slight movement of her eyelids.

"You have decided to join me," Jario exclaimed in a nasty tone.

She sat up feeling her hands restrained and looked around not recognizing her surroundings. Seeing Jario, she tried to flash back to the castle, but nothing happened. He saw her look of surprise and laughed.

"Your powers do not work in the Canyon of Obscurity, My Lady," he responded, as he walked closer to her.

"What do you want from me?" she asked, with fear in her eyes.

"I don't want anything from you," he replied, as he shook his head. "I want to rule Evergreen Castle. With you as my mate, I will be the master. You can willingly stand by my side as my mate, or I can force you. The choice is yours."

She fell back upon the bed and turned her face toward the wall.

Thomas must be hunting for me, she thought, as she tried to reach his thoughts seeing nothing but darkness.

Jario knew that daylight would be upon them soon and the cracked and shattered windows presented a problem for both of them. Looking about the room, there wasn't much left behind by the Wispets. He found a few small tattered blankets and hung them over the broken shutters. Shoving the door upright, he was able to close it securely. The idea of spending the day in the small storage closet or under the bed sickened him. Knowing the canyon was empty of any living thing, the lack of blood would soon be an issue. They could feed upon each other, but he wanted to save that for when he took her as his mate.

Realizing he hadn't planned for feeding, he pulled the wooden door open and headed for the other side of the canyon toward Whistler River to hunt for animals. He would have to hurry since the sun would rise within a few hours. Securing the door, he sped through the canyon to look for a good place to scale the canyon wall.

Hearing him leave, Lara sat up looking about for anything she might use as a weapon. Losing her powers was a negative, but she still knew how to fight. Finding an old iron hinge that had fallen from the shutter, she reached out with her foot as far as she could. Pointing the toe of her slipper it was just out of her reach. She stood and pulled on the ropes that were tied to the bed. The bed moved toward her slightly. Pulling once more, she saw it move a few inches more. Stretching her foot out again, she was able to put the toe of her slipper on the hinge and drag it toward her. Bending down she was stopped just short of reaching it by the ropes that bound her hands. Sitting back on the bed, frustration started to control her. Taking a deep breath, she stretched and placed her feet on either side of the hinge. Sliding her feet together she was able to scoot the hinge up between the bottoms of her slippers. Lifting her feet, she grabbed the hinge. Looking it over it appeared to be solid and had a sharp point made more for decoration but would be useful as a weapon. She hid it under the mattress and sat back down feeling more confident. Seeing the marks she had made on the floor, she knew that Jario would notice them and wonder what she had found. Looking around for something to cover the marks, she saw the thick dust that rested upon the coverlet of the bed. She stood and carefully pulled the coverlet from the bed. Shaking the dust from the coverlet over the marks seemed to make them blend in more and not be so noticeable. Pleased that she had covered her find, she spread the coverlet back on the bed and sat back hoping that Thomas would find her soon.

Chapter 17

Rushing through the doorway of the Command Center, Tate shouted, "I need help!" He stood holding her body securely against his chest. Feeling her struggle to breathe, he lightly kissed her forehead as he pleaded, "Gavenia, please stay with me. Don't give up. I'm getting help for you." He heard the sound of running. Looking up, he saw Preston and Camilla enter the room. "She needs help. She's dying," Tate yelled franticly. He felt tears begin to fill his eyes.

Moving closer, Preston saw her bruised and bloody body. "Get Flora," he ordered Camilla. She immediately turned and ran from the Command Center. "Follow me. We'll meet Flora in the Healing Room."

Tate followed Preston through the hallways clutching Gavenia's body securely to his chest. Stepping into the room lined with cots, he knelt down and placed her carefully on the clean linen. Hearing her moan and gasp for air, he gently brushed the strands of bloody hair from her face with his fingers, hoping to see her open her eyes.

"You are safe now, Gavenia," whispered Tate. "You are safe. Flora will help you."

Flora entered the room ordering everyone out. Refusing to leave her, Tate stood and backed to the open doorway. The warmth he had felt when he held her against his chest was gone the moment he stopped touching her. Bending over Gavenia, Flora touched the pulse at her neck. For a moment, he thought she had left them until Flora turned her head toward him and softly said, "She is still alive but very weak." She carefully removed the saturated tunic revealing the numerous slashes and bite marks that covered her discolored body. Tate gasped from the sight of her mutilated body. He could now see the full extent of the torture inflicted by Magna and Jario.

Filling a bowl with water, Flora gently swirled her hand within the water to warm it. Dipping a cloth into the warm water, she began to wash Gavenia's face. Hearing a slight whimper, Tate moved forward in a protective stance.

"Back off," Flora sneered, looking over her shoulder at him. "This will surely hurt her. There is not a place upon her body that is free from torture. Her skin is raw and full of infection, but I must get her clean before she can start to heal."

Tate relaxed and backed toward the door. "I am sorry," he whispered. "I saw her tortured over and over and could do nothing to stop it. I don't want her to feel any more pain."

Flora smiled acknowledging his concern and turned her focus back to Gavenia. "I will do my best to keep from hurting her," she replied, as she continued to wash the blood from Gavenia's battered face. "Now, get out of here and leave me to my work so I can help this poor woman."

Tate nodded and backed away from the door. Taking one last look at Gavenia, he left in search of Thomas.

* * *

Seeing Preston posting maps on the wall of the Command Center, he looked around for Thomas. Tate looked back at Preston and asked, "Have you seen Thomas?"

"I saw Lady Lara and Thomas making their way to the stables just after sunset," he replied. He continued to hammer the maps into place. "Elda was with them."

A dreadful howling sound echoed about the room coming from outside through the open door. Preston and Tate grabbed a sword and ran in the direction of the stables. They could see Thomas kneeling in the pasture with his dagger drawn, and Elda stood with her sword held above her head.

Tolin ran from the stables hearing the horrible sound and shouted, "What has happened?"

Thomas heard his brother running toward him as he stood facing Elda's paralyzed body. He looked at his brother and then back at Elda.

"Thomas, what has happened to Lady Lara?" Preston shouted.

"He has taken her!" Thomas shouted. "He has taken her! A man has vanished with Lady Lara! I could do nothing to stop him."

The men huddled around Elda and tried to remove her sword from her hands. It stood firm within her grasp, and they were unable to remove it. Elda could see the men standing about her. She heard their voices, but she could not move. She had seen the tall man take hold of Lady Lara's hand. She saw her eyes close as he pulled her next to his body, wrapping his arm around her waist. She heard the few words he spoke and watched as they vanished right before her eyes.

She was unable to do anything to save her. He had paralyzed her.

"Elda, can you hear us?" Preston asked, as he looked into her eyes for some kind of reaction. Placing his hand upon her shoulder, he felt the solid nature of her stance. She was cold to the touch. "Elda, can you move?"

"The man must have used his power to cause this," said Thomas. "He looked familiar to me, but I don't know where I would have seen him." Searching his mind for who he might be, he suddenly stopped as the memory of pain shot through his body. "I know who he is," Thomas grabbed Tate's arm to steady himself. "He is the vampire that turned me." He clinched his fists as he thought of that night. Worry for Lara's safety and what he might do to her, filled his mind.

"If he is a vampire, he must be working with Jario," Preston responded. "This is no coincidence. We hear of Jario's plot and this happens. He must have taken her to him. It is the only thing that makes sense. The army is searching for Jario. When we find him, surely we will find Lady Lara."

"Did he say anything?" Tate asked Thomas.

Looking up, Thomas nodded as he looked back at Elda, still frozen in place. "It is just a favor," replied Thomas. "I thought his comment strange, but he was telling us he wasn't taking her for himself. I am sure of it."

This verified to everyone that he was working for someone. They believed that someone to be Jario. After Tate and Preston had seen what Magna and Jario had done to Gavenia, they knew they had to find Lady Lara quickly.

Slowly Elda could feel her hand warm and begin to move. Unable to securely grasp her sword, its weight caused it to fall from her hand to the grass.

"She is coming out of it," sighed Thomas, as he bent to retrieve her sword.

After a few more moments, Elda was able to drop her arm to her side. It wasn't long until she could move completely on her own. Appearing to stagger, Tate took her arm and helped steady her.

Tate asked, "Do you feel any pain?"

As Elda tried to move her feet, she saw the ground swirl beneath her and she began to sway. Tate gripped her tightly around her waist to keep her from falling. Seeing more than one of him, she smiled. Closing her eyes, she waited for the strange feeling to leave her.

"Did he hurt you? Do you feel any pain?" Tate asked, again.

"No," replied Elda as her temper flared. "I care not for myself. I have failed Lady Lara. I could not protect her." Clenching her fists, she stomped her boot against the ground and felt Tate's arm leave her body. "He threw a spell or power at me before I could do anything to stop him," she spoke through gritted teeth. "I saw him, and if I saw him again, I would surely recognize him."

Seeing Elda start to stumble, Tate grabbed her arm to keep her from falling. She bent forward and put her hands on her knees trying to release the dizzy feeling.

"I will take you to see Flora," Tate said, as he watched Elda straighten. "She may be able to heal what remains of the spell." Still unsteady on her feet, he continued to hold Elda's arm as they walked back to the Command Center.

"We have to find her," Thomas said, as he followed behind them.

* * *

Lara had heard Jario running toward the cottage through the dry underbrush. She had hoped that Thomas or the army would have found her while he was away hunting, but there had been no sign of them. After sitting up, she checked under the mattress to make sure her new weapon was still safely tucked away. The sun was just starting to come up as Jario stepped through the doorway caring the limp carcass of a goat. He glanced her way as he dropped it onto the stone floor.

Opening and closing the cupboard doors, he looked for a cup or anything that would hold the goat's blood. Finding small wooden bowls, he sat them on the floor next to the goat. Picking up the goat by the head, he drew his dagger from his boot and sliced the goat's throat. Carefully holding the goat, he watched as the red liquid ran freely from the goat's throat into the wooden bowls. Once they were full, he walked toward Lara handing her a bowl.

"Drink," he said sternly. "I don't want my mate starving."

Lara took the bowl without offering a response and put the bowl to her mouth. She closed her eyes and drank until the bowl was empty. Jario emptied his bowl in a gulp and grabbed the empty bowl from her throwing them onto the floor.

"Now that the sun has risen, we will sleep," Jario smirked, as he sat down to remove his boots. He stood and slipped his leather belt from his waist and pulled his tunic over his head revealing his hard muscular chest. Walking toward Lara he ordered, "Lie down on your side and face the wall."

"No! You are not sharing this cot," she said, angry that he would think of doing such a thing. "I will not allow it."

"I am not asking," he said sternly, as he pointed to the wall. "Do as I say! You have no power over me, Lara." He watched her turn her face away from him. "I am your master, now."

Jario slowly untied the leather laces from his breeches and watched her eyes as he began to pull them down over his thighs. He smirked as Lara quickly brought her feet up on the cot and laid back turning her face toward the wall. Feeling his desire for her, he let his breeches fall to the floor and moved toward the cot.

She heard his breeches hit the floor and felt the shifting of the cot as the weight of his body pressed into it. She could feel his chest press against her back, and it made her shoulders shiver in disgust. As he ran his hand down her arm and along her hip, she could hear him drag his tongue across his fangs.

"You will find that I can be a gentle lover. I can spend forever, kissing the most intimate parts of your body. If you prefer something with a bit more brutality, you need only ask," he said with his mouth next to her ear. Letting his tongue flick her earlobe, he heard her small gasp and smiled. "It is up to you which lover I become."

Lara gasped as she felt his hand pull the hem of her dress up and his rough hand caress her leg. Holding perfectly still, she felt him drawing small circles upon her thigh and his body pressing tightly against her back. Finally pulling his hand away, she heard him laugh.

"I won't take you now, my sweet," Jario whispered. "I am tired from hunting and my body needs to rest. There is plenty of time for me to enjoy caressing your body." He wrapped his arm around her waist and pulled her tighter against his naked body.

Lara could feel his body drift into deep slumber. She closed her eyes and leaned as close to the wall as she could. She knew she had escaped Jario's advances this time, but it was clear that he intended on having her.

Could Meadow have been wrong about Thomas becoming her mate, she thought?

It was clear that Jario's intentions were to mate and become the master of Evergreen Castle. Again, she tried to read the thoughts of Thomas and saw nothing but darkness. Sighing with disappointment, she drew a "T" into the palm of her hand with her finger and brought it to her lips. Kissing her palm she silently said, "Thomas, I love you."

Chapter 18

The maps that hung on the wall in the Command Center had been marked for the locations that Tate had searched and not found Jario. The other commands had not been heard from and did not know that Lady Lara had been kidnapped. The messenger hawks had been readied by Tolin and sent to relay the bad news that their Lady had been kidnapped. They were requested to report back on the areas they had searched.

The army gathered around Tate as he told them of entering the Black Thistle Castle and finding Gavenia in the dungeon cell alone. He attempted to describe the glimmer of the spell he had seen surrounding the castle after crossing the drawbridge and the fear they felt with the sudden appearance of Magna. He was agitated, and his arms moved wildly, as he explained how Magna had grabbed his arm and tried to flash him back into the castle. They listened to him recount how he had been able to make "Hands of Fire" for the first time. They all laughed when they heard how it had caused her arm to separate from her body before she vanished back into the castle. Preston knew that Tate was lucky to have gotten away from Magna. After listening to Tate, Preston reminded everyone that more caution was to be used when approaching Jario, since one touch from him could turn them to stone.

Thomas was proud of his brother. Tate was strong and very brave. He had taken a risk to save Gavenia and succeeded. After visiting the Healing Room with Tate, he had seen firsthand the grave condition of Gavenia and feared the same fate for his Lara. Thomas paced as he thought of the danger that could befall Lara.

His Lara, he thought. I promise to save you like you saved me.

He stepped away and turned his back to the group huddled around the map. Concentrating only on Lara, he pulled his vision to search for her.

Give me a glimpse of where she is, or let me see that she is unharmed, he thought, as a blurry vision of something started to form and then became nothing but darkness.

Running his hands through his hair in frustration, he turned and walked back toward the group.

Looking up at the map, Thomas glanced at the area surrounding Black Thistle Castle. "If he isn't at Black Thistle Castle, he has to be someplace where Lady Lara cannot use her powers. Otherwise, she would have flashed back to the castle," he said to Preston, looking for suggestions on where to look for her. "Where could Jario take her and keep her from using her powers?" Preston studied the large map and pointed to a location near the castle.

"The Canyon of Obscurity blocks gifted powers, however, it would also block Jario's powers," replied Preston.

Elda listened carefully to the conversation and stepped forward from the doorway. She had recovered from the spell and was steady on her feet. "Unless someone is helping him hide her," Elda said, as she thought back to the man that had taken Lady Lara. "I was paralyzed and could not use my powers or even talk. The man that took her must be controlling her powers."

Seeing Tate, Elda nodded her thanks for helping her to the Healing Room. After seeing Gavenia in the cot next to her, she knew that he must be struggling to keep his mind on finding Lara.

Thinking back to the moment Lara vanished, Thomas remembered the words the man spoke. "The stranger said, this is just a favor," Thomas stated. "It was said as if he meant no harm and only took her to receive payment from a favor or bargain. Who makes favors or bargains?" He looked among the others waiting for an answer.

"Well, the only others powerful enough to make bargains are Meadow and Velsa," Elda replied. "Meadow would never hurt Lady Lara. She was just a small child when Lady Lara found her and brought her here to the castle. It has to be the Black Magic Witch, Velsa." Elda shook her head fearing a confrontation with Velsa would turn out badly. "Even if she knows anything, she won't tell us unless she receives something in return."

Anxious to find the witch, Velsa, Thomas looked relieved that they might have a way to find Lara. "We have to try," said Thomas, as he approached the map to have someone show him where he could find the witch.

After going through all the suggested possibilities, it was decided that Thomas and Tate would make the journey to the witch's cottage since they could travel both day and night. As they readied their swords across their backs, strapped daggers to their legs and tucked additional daggers in their boots, they left the castle hoping to find the witch cooperative.

Seeing Thomas and Tate leave, Preston took another look at the map. He turned to Elda and ordered, "Take a few men and head down to the docks. The man you saw isn't a regular around here, and he may be getting ready to leave on the ship in the harbor. This stranger may be too powerful to capture, but you may find men that know of him and can offer us useful information."

"We will go with you," Baxter said, as he looked at Oliver. Oliver nodded and both men retrieved their weapons. Once ready, Baxter and Oliver double checked their weapons were secure and followed Elda as they headed for the docks.

* * *

The crew were busy hauling supplies from the wagons up the ramp to the deck of the ship when Elda spotted the sails. They waited to approach a wagon that had departed from the dock after having their goods unloaded. Elda stepped from the side of the dirt road waving her hand in greeting to a slender man and asked, "Do you have a moment, sir? Can you tell me where the ship is headed?" The man slowed his wagon, cautiously held up his horses and removed his hat.

"It leaves tomorrow morning, but I don't know where it is bound," he stated. "I bring my load of root vegetables for the coin and don't care where they take them."

Elda nodded her thanks and let the man go on about his business seeing another empty wagon not far behind.

Spotting Zeb, from the tavern, sitting at the reins, she smiled and waved as she said, "I see Lulu let you out alone tonight."

Zeb slowed his wagon and gave her a big grin. He laughed and removed his hat, setting it on the bench beside him.

"She let me out to collect payment for a load of ale," he replied knowing Elda knew exactly who really ran the tavern. He always enjoyed seeing Elda. He thought she was too pretty to be in the vampire's army. She had frequently helped him and his wife with rowdy men that came ashore looking for trouble.

"I have a question for you. If you feel uncomfortable about answering, I understand," she said, giving him a serious look.

"Ask away, sweetie," he responded, laughing. "We are friends, Elda. If I can help you like you have helped me, then I will give it a try."

Elda smiled and asked, "Have you seen a tall man with long silver hair in the tavern lately?"

Nodding, he grinned and responded, "Yes, I sure have seen that man. He was a creepy fellow with strange sounding words. He is not from around these parts. He was in the tavern a few times, and Jario came in and sat down at his table. One of those nights, they up and left together. I saw the man on the deck of the ship tonight. Does that help you?"

Elda smiled knowing, with Zeb's help, they had made the connection to Jario. Yes it does," she replied. "You have done us a great service. Now get on out of here before Lulu comes looking for you."

Zeb nodded with a smile and gave the horses a quick cluck with his tongue. "Don't be a stranger. Come see us. Lulu would enjoy your company," he smiled and gave her a wink. He grabbed his cap and secured it on his bold head as he headed on down the road.

Hearing everything Zeb had told Elda, Baxter and Oliver came out of the bushes ready to head for the docks. They knew he was on the ship, but they didn't know if he still had Lady Lara or if he had passed her on to Jario. Odds were that Jario had her hidden somewhere.

Baxter asked Elda, "Do you want to board the ship and look around? We have time before she sails."

She stood silently for a moment before she spoke, "My gut is telling me that she isn't on the ship. If he paralyzed her like he did me, he would have to stay with her since it doesn't last long. He couldn't leave her unattended. I say we let him go and focus on finding Jario."

Baxter agreed and pointed in the direction of the tavern as he said, "We might get lucky at the tavern and find someone that knows of the mystery man's talents." Agreeing, they walked back down the road away from the docks toward the tavern.

The smell of ale and body odor was strong and the tavern was crowded. The room appeared to be full of men consuming their wages received from the ship's captain. Looking about the room, the tables were full and left the rail of the bar their only option. Lulu saw them and eagerly waved them over.

Filling three mugs with ale, she sat them down in front of the trio and shouted over the noise, "They are on the house!"

Oliver was the first to pick up his mug and turned to look about the room as he drank the strong liquid. Spying a lass that he knew, he wandered over and gave her a slap on the rump, as he barked, "Have you missed me, lass?"

She jumped and flung her arms around his neck. She stepped back and tilted her head motioning toward the stairs of the tavern. Seeing him nod, she took his hand and led him upstairs.

Elda shook her head and loudly complained so Oliver could hear, "We aren't here to press the feathers; we need answers. There has to be someone in this tavern that knows something about this man, and you won't find it upstairs."

Two hours later, Oliver came down the stairs with a grin from ear to ear. He walked up to the bar and ordered another ale. He could see from the expression on Elda's face that she was furious with him. Seeing the large cup of ale set in front of him, he grabbed it and took a big gulp quenching the dryness in his throat.

Wiping the foam from his mouth with his sleeve, he said, "His name is Balgair. He comes to town on the big ships to bring Velsa supplies. The lass told me he can make lots of magic and can even take magic from other vampires. With powers like that, he must be a collector."

Listening carefully, Elda asked, "How did she find out all this information about him?"

Oliver took another large gulp of ale. Starting to laugh, he continued, "He told her one night upstairs. He thought he had wiped her memories when he was ready to leave her bed. She was tired of losing her memories and asked Meadow for a blocking spell last year. I figure she might be full of all kinds of information, and I may have to come back now and then."

Hearing enough about his bodily desires, Elda pushed the mugs back away from the men indicating it was time to leave.

Once outside the tavern, Baxter laughed until his sides ached. "I can't believe that you got all that information out of that pretty little lass. What did you have to promise her?" He looked at Oliver and punched him in the gut with his elbow.

"I will never tell," smirked Oliver. "But, if I was still a human, I would be smoking a good pipe right now and thinking about the promises I made to her."

They all laughed and headed back to the castle. Not waiting for Baxter to slow them down, Oliver picked him up and threw him over his shoulder as they ran full speed back to the Command Center to share the new information they had obtained.

Chapter 19

"I feel like we have been walking around in circles," said Tate. He stumbled over some roots embedded in the forest floor. They were hidden by dried leaves causing plump frogs to leap for shelter after their hiding places were revealed. "It has to be around here somewhere." Seeing another fog leap over a dried log, Tate asked, "How many of these small creatures do you think keep the old witch company?"

The sun had been out for some time, but very little of the light filtered through the thick tangled cover of the tree's branches. They knew they were in the right area based on the map in the Command Center, but there had been no sight of the witch's cottage.

Turning toward the sound of a squawking bird, a distant patch of trees began to fade and slowly disappear. There, barely visible through the remaining trees, stood a small cottage where there had been nothing but trees.

Thomas looked at Tate dumbfounded and asked, "Didn't we just come from there?"

Walking quietly toward the cottage, they could smell the smoke from the stack above the roof. Stepping to the door, Tate pounded his fist firmly against the wooden door. They were answered with complete silence.

Pounding again, they heard a raspy voice holler, "What do you want, vampires? I am an old lady, and you have disturbed my nap."

Many stories had been told of the old witch. The one most repeated was how she had won the War of the Witches. She was a powerful witch that no one ever crossed without some kind of ramification. Looking at Tate, Thomas nervously held onto his resolve.

"We are hunting for Lady Lara," Thomas shouted leaning toward the crack in the door. "She has been taken by a stranger, and we thought you might be willing to help us."

The door slowly opened offering a pungent smell of drying herbs and smoke from her hearth.

"Come in young vampires," she replied. "Come in and make yourselves comfortable."

Entering the cottage, the men looked about the cluttered room searching for Velsa as the door closed behind them. Seeing her leisurely rocking back and forth in her chair by the fire, Thomas felt hesitant but anxious to speak with the old witch.

"Don't be shy," smirked Velsa, as she patted a wooden stool that sat beside her. "I won't bite, like others I know of within this room."

Tate couldn't help but laugh. The old woman had a wicked sense of humor. She gave Tate a wink and a toothless smile after hearing his laughter at her comment.

Making his way through the bundles that were still tied in burlap and stacked upon the floor, he ducked his head to avoid the hanging herbs. He straddled the low milking stool and carefully sat down placing his hand upon the floor for balance.

"I have come to ask for your help," he said, with a nervous tone to his voice as he grasped the witch's hands that were folded in her lap. "Lady Lara has been taken by a stranger, and we are desperate to find her."

Velsa starred at his hands covering hers and shivered from the contact. She gently pulled them away from his grasp as she looked up noticing his striking silver-gray eyes. Thomas sat back afraid that he had offended the witch. He tucked his hands back into his lap and waited for a reply.

She tilted her head and squinted her eyes wondering what he knew and asked, "Do you know who took your lady?"

Nodding, Thomas responded quickly, "He was a tall man with silver hair. He spoke of a favor before he disappeared with her."

Velsa suddenly stood. Clenching her hands into fists, she paced in a circle speaking in a tongue that he had never heard. Blue sparks flew around the room and Tate ducked as one flew past his ear just missing him. It was apparent to both men that she knew the stranger they described.

"Balgair is your stranger," she hissed. She flung another batch of blue sparks around the room. Pulling at her hair, she grumbled and turned to spit into the flames of the hearth. More sparks flew about the room, and Tate stayed tucked behind a crate out of the path of her agitated display. Throwing her shoulders back, she closed her eyes and calmed herself.

"He and I do business with one another. Balgair brings me supplies that I need and cannot find in my forest. I fear he has meddled where he should not have meddled. He will know my scorn the next time he comes to see me."

Velsa smacked her hand against the stones of the hearth making more sparks fly about the cottage. Causing the hanging herbs to smolder, Tate looked worried the cottage would soon be fully engulfed from Velsa's temper and made note of a path to the door.

"He does nothing as a favor, unless, he obtains payment. His desired payment is the gifted powers of others. He is known to the witches as the Silver Fox or the Power Collector. He is becoming almost as powerful as the witches and has absolutely no fear of other vampires."

She walked over to her table and picked up a tattered black velvet box. Lifting the lid, she pulled out an orb holding a shimmering brightness inside and held it in the palm of her hand. Mumbling a few words under her breath, she studied something that appeared inside the bright orb. Circling her finger over the brightness, the picture changed.

Placing the orb back into the velvet box, she then turned and said, "Balgair does not have your Lady Lara. He is on a ship ready to sail out of the harbor. I don't expect him back until he brings my next load of supplies. It will be several months before he returns."

Thomas felt some relief, but he knew if this Balgair didn't have Lara then he must have taken her to someone else. The obvious choice was Jario.

Raking his hands over his face, he looked up at the witch and asked, "Can you tell me where she is? Can you help us? I suspect that this Balgair has taken Lady Lara to Jario."

The witch looked at Thomas and sighed deeply calming herself as she returned to her chair by the fire.

"If I tell you where you can find Jario, I will expect a payment for the favor," she said, with hopeful curiosity in her expression.

Tate pulled her attention away from Thomas, as he stood up and stepped over the crates. Raising her eyebrow, Tate decided not to move and stood perfectly still.

"I will pay anything," responded Thomas. He looked at Tate and back at the witch. "I need to find her. I will do anything."

Velsa smiled knowing she would have anything she wanted from him. "I fear love has made you hasty with your response, but I accept," she said, as she drew her hand along the side of Thomas' face. "You are very handsome. I adore the silver-gray of your eyes."

Thomas waited for her to continue, but he was afraid of what she meant by her last comment.

"Jario was a visitor of my cottage not long ago," she said, as she continued to caress his face.

Feeling the hardness of her yellowed nails against his skin made him tense, but he did nothing in hopes he would find out where to find Jario and possibly Lara. He watched her close her eyes as she stroked the side of his face, over and over.

"He wanted safe passage into the Canyon of Obscurity and to retain his powers once inside the canyon. I granted him his favor for only five days and a payment of my terms. He willingly accepted," she said, as she opened her eyes.

Velsa stood withdrawing her hands from his face. She hesitated for a moment looking at Thomas, as if she felt pity for the young vampire and might change her mind. Shaking her head and closing her eyes, she began to chant.

Several items within the cottage began to move about the room, and flashes of light bounced from wall to wall and played with her outstretched hands. Thomas could feel his body tense and a slight burning sensation within his eyes. Closing his eyes, he could feel them pulse to flashes of light. As the burning stopped, he opened his eyes, and the lights within the cottage dimmed. It seemed to get darker and darker until he could no longer see his hand in front of his face. Thomas tried to focus his eyes in the dark, but he couldn't see a thing.

He was hesitant but quietly asked, "Why is it so dark? Did you put the fire out?"

Velsa picked up something from her table, and Thomas heard a clasp open and then a moment later it was closed.

"Your payment has been collected and you are free to go," she said, with a sigh of satisfaction in her voice.

"But, I can't see," he franticly replied, as he carefully touched his eyes with his fingers. "Something must have gone wrong. I can't see."

Tate moved quickly toward Thomas taking his arm and bending to look at his eyes and then at the witch.

As he looked up at Velsa, she smiled and said, "He said he would pay anything. He made his payment of the silver-gray color of his eyes. It has left him blind. I am sorry, but I loved the color of his eyes and could not keep myself from taking them."

Fury rose in Tate as he looked at Thomas standing in shock. Pulling his dagger, Tate stepped toward Velsa just as she disappeared in a swirling wisp of blue smoke. "That damn witch," he said. "She'll pay for this."

Leading Thomas through the cottage and out into the forest, Tate feared they would never be able to find Jario.

"What were you thinking? We should have never trusted that hag," shouted Tate as he clutched his brother's arm.

"Tate, take me to the canyon," Thomas pleaded with the sound of resolve still in his voice. "I have to find her. If I have to do it blind, I will."

Reluctantly, Tate led Thomas through the forest heading for the Canyon of Obscurity and the army commands that had been sent in search of Jario.

Chapter 20

The room was swathed in darkness, and a familiar canyon breeze blew through the worn blankets that covered the windows. Waking before Jario, she kept her body as still as possible. She feared what he would do, if she should wake him. He hadn't hurt her yet, but he was clearly frustrated. She had heard of his temper from the other members of her army. Lara had made up her mind she would try to do whatever he wanted to keep him calm, anything but mating with him or drinking human blood. Feeling his arm move, she knew he was waking and closed her eyes pretending to still be asleep.

Feeling the cool breeze blow against his back, Jario opened his eyes resting his gaze upon Lara's hair that was beginning to loosen from its braid. Strands of strawberry blonde hair brushed against his face. He ran his hand along the rise of her hip and felt her tense knowing she was awake and only pretending to be asleep. He gently pulled her braid away from her neck and lightly pressed his lips against her skin. She clinched her fingers making fists as he began dragging his fangs against the back of her neck. As a few beads of blood appeared where he had broken the skin, he moved quickly to capture the precious liquid on his tongue. His eyes rolled back as his mouth exploded from the instant feeling of sensual pleasure that traveled down his body. She could feel his arousal pressing against her lower back and froze.

"Don't worry," he sneered. "As much as I want to, it isn't time to take you yet. I prefer your body willing when we mate."

He raised up and ran the back of his hand across his mouth feeling his thirst for blood pleading with him to take more from her. Forcing himself to ignore the calling, he stood and stretched his arms over his head. Bending down to retrieve his breeches, he walked to the door throwing it open feeling the night air against his naked body. He loved the night and the darkness it brought. Even as a child, he had never been afraid of the dark. Once he was turned, he thrived in the darkness and let it seize every part of him. He even delighted in the fear it brought to others.

Jario turned back to look at Lara facing the wall. "I will have a surprise for you later tonight," he said, as he pulled on his breeches and sat to tug on his boots. "It might not be to your liking, but I'm sure you will change your mind eventually." He pulled his tunic over his head and headed back to the door. "Don't go anywhere," he laughed, as he left the cottage securing the door behind him.

Feeling a great sense of relief, Lara sat up and stretched the best she could with her hands tied to the bed. Sleep had been difficult, and her body felt stiff from resting in one position unable to move. Smelling him on her clothes and on the bedding, she longed to wash his scent from her body. She pulled at the ropes as she tried to release herself from her restraints to no avail. Without her powers, she was now weak and helpless against Jario's promised advances. Frustrated, tears slipped from her eyes as she thought of Thomas and how much she missed him. She was sure Thomas, along with others, would be searching for her and would find her soon. She had waited over two hundred years for him, she could wait a little longer. Again she tried to reach his thoughts, but sadly, her attempts offered nothing but darkness.

"I know you will come for me," she said. "Thomas, please find me and soon. I fear the things he will do to me."

* * *

Speeding through the dead remains of the canyon floor, Jario headed for a small village. He had seen it from a distance the previous evening. It was nestled against the mountains on the other side of the canyon along the Whistler River. He had stolen the goat from a farmer's pen on the outskirts of the village, but was determined that they would not be drinking goat blood tonight. Pulling himself up the crags of the canyon wall, he sensed his plan was working. It gave him a strong feeling of empowerment and made him even more anxious to return to the Evergreen Castle as their master. Just one thing stood in the way and that was Lady Lara. He would change her mind. If not tonight, he would have to change her mind soon.

Reaching the center of the village, he noticed a small tavern with candles burning brightly in the colored glass panes of the windows. He could hear singing and laughter. The closer he got to the thick wooden door, the more he could sense and smell human blood. Making his way into the tavern, he looked about for a place to sit. Seeing that he didn't recognize anyone made him sigh with relief.

A young woman stood leaning against the wooden rail of the bar.

She was tall and thin with dark curls about her face. Her skin was the color of strong coffee laden with heavy cream.

Seeing him, she approached the table where he sat and asked, "Good evening, what can I bring you?"

Jario raked his eyes up and down the woman. His eyes stopped to linger on her full breasts bulging from the top of her apron. Licking his lips, he looked up at the young woman.

"Ale, if you have it," he said, smiling and giving her a wink and tossing a coin on the small wooden table.

Winking back, she turned and made her way through the crowd swaying her hips for his benefit. Leaning against the railing, she placed the order and then turned to look over her shoulder at him. Jario licked his lips overtly for her to see. Caught looking at him, she blushed and turned to retrieve the large cup of ale. She made her way back to his table never breaking eye contact.

"One ale," she said, as she bent down to retrieve the coin and show more of her cleavage. "Can I get you anything else?"

Jario brought the cup to his mouth. He licked the foam that ran down the side of the vessel as he watched her tremble slightly, smelling her arousal. "This will do for now," he said, as he placed another coin on the table.

She snatched the coin and put it in the pocket of her apron.

"Just give me a wave when you are ready for another," she said, as she turned away heading back to the bar.

Jario watched her move about the tavern serving ale and food to the men sitting about the small room. She was friendly with the men and seemed to know most of them by name. Every now and then, she looked in his direction. He could smell the blood that ran beneath her skin, and it called to him. Waiting long enough, he saw her look his way, and he waved indicating that he wanted more ale. She hurried to the bar to retrieve another cup of ale for him.

Making her way to his table, she could feel her heart quicken with excitement. This man was handsome in a dangerous looking way and seemed to be interested in her.

Setting the ale down and picking up the coin, she asked, "Will you be needing a room here at the tavern?"

"I am only here for a meal and a cup of ale," he offered, loud enough for men at the other table to hear. "I'm on my way to the harbor to sail to parts unknown."

Her eyes grew wide with excitement.

"How exciting it must be to travel to places you have never seen before," she said, as she thought of her dreams of leaving her village. "I have always dreamed of seeing other villages.

"Would you like to come along?" he asked surprising her. "We could explore the world together." Laughing at first, he paused slightly showing her an expression of embarrassment and continued, "Forgive me, I am being too bold. You must be married. The ale has made me rude."

She shook her head and replied, "I have never been married. I would love to leave this place and see what the world has to offer." She looked at him carefully and asked, "Are you teasing me?"

Jario smiled knowing he had her in his trap. "No. I do not tease you. Bring me a meal of bread and cheese," he said. "Once I have finished my meal, I will wait for you to pack your things, if you are willing to follow me." Reaching in his pocket, he retrieved several coins. "Here are a few coins to pay for my food, drink and some extra to pay for a basket of bread and cheese to carry with us."

She smiled and snatched the coins and scurried back to the kitchen to prepare his meal and their basket for the trip. Going upstairs to her tiny room, she tied her few belongings into a bundle for the journey. She carried them back downstairs and stowed them behind the bar.

Finished with his meal, Jario signaled the young woman that he was ready to leave. She untied her apron and threw it on the surface of the bar.

Grabbing the small bundle she had tucked behind the bar and her freshly packed basket, she turned to the man behind the bar and shouted, "I'm off to see the world and never coming back to this filthy little village."

She followed Jario happily out the door and into the night. They walked for what seemed like hours. The night was cool, and she stopped to pull a shawl from her small bundle.

"How far is the ship?" she asked, as she was already tired and her feet were starting to ache.

Jario knew he had to play along until he had her in the canyon. There, he could compel her and get her easily back to the cottage.

"It is a short distance beyond the canyon. I will help you down to the canyon floor and up the other side. I know this canyon well and have found paths that are not too steep to take in the dark. Do not be afraid. I will help you," he responded with a note of concern for her wellbeing in his voice. "Remember, this is our adventure. It will be fun to do things together."

She smiled pulling her shawl around her shoulders. Picking up her bundle, she continued to walk beside Jario. He told her about the beautiful places he had seen and stories about unusual people he had met. She was amazed at how much he knew about the world and was eager to see everything he wanted to show her. Finally reaching the canyon's edge, she looked out over the width of the canyon and saw little but darkness.

"Are you sure this will be safe?" she asked, as she thought she might change her mind. Tempted to turn and head back to the tavern, she felt Jario touch her hand.

"Take my hand and follow behind me," Jario said, as he took her belongings in one hand and gently took her hand with the other. "Don't be afraid, I won't let you fall. Watch where I step, and step where I have stepped. We will be down in no time at all."

She placed her other hand around his wrist feeling more secure holding on with both hands, as they made their way down the steep side of the canyon. Losing her balance and slipping a few times, he always caught her securely with his hand and kept her safe, making her trust him completely. Slowly they made their way down to the bottom.

"I can't believe I did that," she gasped, sitting on the canyon floor to calm her nerves and regain her breath. "The trail was very steep. You kept me from falling."

The moon was out and provided enough light to see the outlines of trees and rocks. Looking around, she could see shadows made from moving branches causing the canyon to seem alive. Afraid, she stood and put her arms around Jario's waist for protection.

Jario looked down into her eyes to compel her as he slowly said, "You are under my control and will do as I say. You no longer have a voice."

She wobbled slightly and then stood perfectly still looking up at Jario. He picked her up and threw her over his shoulder and sped through the canyon floor back to the cottage.

Lara heard the sound of someone running and the door burst open. In stepped Jario with a woman thrown over his shoulder. He dropped a bundle at the door and then set a basket on the table.

Turning to face Lara, he said, with a smirk on his face, "I've brought you a guest for dinner."

Chapter 21

Navigating slowly through the forest, Tate held Thomas by the arm as they made their way into the command's camp. Tate could see Will sharpening his blade and waved his arm to draw his attention.

Will saw the pair and started running toward them as he yelled, "I told the command about the spell at Black Thistle Castle and how you burned Magna's arm off. They were all sorry they missed it."

Tate nodded and guided Thomas to a small boulder to sit.

Seeing that Thomas needed help, Will asked, "What happened to him?"

"That damn witch, Velsa, took his eyesight," he responded in a frustrated tone. "Thomas made a bargain with the old hag before he knew what she wanted in return."

Thomas tried to stand but stumbled. He reached for Tate's arm to steady himself.

Feeling his temper flare as he shouted, "Enough about my eyes. So, I'm blind. It won't stop me searching for Lara. Get me to that damn canyon."

Leaving Thomas to rest, Tate joined the other members of the army and explained everything they had heard from the witch. It left no other option but to enter the canyon to kill or capture Jario. Hopefully, they would find Lady Lara and bring her back to Evergreen Castle. It would be a difficult task for everyone. The cliffs were treacherous for humans, but vampires without powers could suffer the same difficulty once they entered the canyon. Informing the command that Jario had bargained to keep his powers made them realize they would be at a great disadvantage. Their only advantage, now, were the numbers. Jario couldn't fight everyone at once. If he used his haze, he could hide himself but not Lady Lara. They would easily be able to see her movement. If he ran leaving her behind, it would allow them to retrieve her and return to the castle. This was the option they all preferred.

Hearing the discussions, Thomas made his way over to the group. "I am going with you, so, you may as well let me in on the plan," Thomas responded, as he put his arm out finding Tate's shoulder.

"You'll never be able to maneuver the cliffs without your sight, and you'll only slow us down," replied Tate. "Let us go, and you stay behind."

Thomas roared as he flailed his arms trying to make contact with anyone. "You won't leave me behind. I have to find her. She is in danger," he shouted. Thomas could feel his arms being lowered and held at his side.

"You'll put everyone else in danger by going," Tate pleaded with Thomas to understand. "If we take you and you lag behind, you will be left behind. We cannot afford to have men watching after you when we need them to fight Jario."

"Agreed, I will find my own way," Thomas nodded his head and bent down pulling his dagger from his boot. "Let's get going!"

The small group waited for the sun to set. Making their way out of the forest that overlooked the canyon, they met up with the few men that stood watch huddled among the rocks at the canyon's entrance.

Approaching the rocks, the men came out from their post to greet them. When the others spied Thomas, Tate silently shook his head at them and pressed a single finger to his mouth to signal not to ask. Assembling the combined commands, Tate addressed the discoveries made at the witch's cottage, again, for the benefit of those that did not know all that had transpired. It was determined that they would divide into two groups. One group to take the left side of the canyon and one to take the right. Thomas would be left to choose which side he would tackle. Not knowing how much of their vampire skills would be available to them, they all decided not to risk jumping off the cliff. A typical soft landing would not be guaranteed.

Pulling the mountain climbing equipment from the trunks used by the humans, they all headed toward the cliff's edge. Tate looked back at his brother and feared this would be the end of him.

Glancing at everyone else, he shouted holding his fist across his chest, "With Honor!" "With Honor," everyone responded as they began to descend the cliffs of the Canyon of Obscurity.

Chapter 22

Jario paced back and forth across the room as he listened to Lara beg for the woman's life. He was sure she thought he was going to torture her, drink from her, and eventually kill her. He laughed out loud knowing she was partially right. He would enjoy drinking her blood and maybe even having some fun with her later, but he would also make Lara drink from her too. If she didn't want her blood, she would go without. He wasn't about to go hunting for more goats to pacify her.

"I have listened to enough of your begging," he angrily addressed her. "I am not going to kill her, at least, not for a few days. She is here to offer us fresh warm blood."

He watched Lara cringe and bring her hands to her mouth as she gasped.

"I won't drink from a human," she shouted, shaking her head. "It will bring the madness to me. I cannot do it. You know the penalty for drinking from a human. My sister was sentenced to a final death for performing such a horrible act."

He knew that madness would follow, but a little madness would make things between them much more interesting.

"You have a choice my dear," he replied. Walking over and kneeling down in front of Lara, he took hold of her hands. Forcing her to look at him, he spoke in a gentle tone, "You can either drink this fine woman's blood or go without the blood you need. How long do you think you will last without it?"

Lara pulled her hands away from him and turned throwing her body down against the coverlet. Running his hand along her hip, Jario closed his eyes thinking of the things he wanted to do to her. Feeling his arousal, he stood and reluctantly walked away from her.

Standing with his back to her he sneered, "Once we are mated, my sweet Lara, and back at the castle, you can have all the goat blood you can drink."

His comment made Lara shiver. She knew it was a matter of time before she had to consume blood. She could not survive without it.

The young woman sat at the table watching Lara cry. She pushed back her chair and fearlessly walked over to Lara. Sitting next to her on the cot, Lara felt her hand stroking her hair trying to comfort her. Lara looked up into the woman's eyes and saw the look of compulsion.

"You have compelled her," she said, through her tears. "She hasn't offered her blood willingly. She is compelled."

Jario laughed and reached for the woman's arm as he pulled her body tightly against his own. He whispered softly into the woman's ear as he watched Lara over her shoulder, "Let me feed on your wrist."

The woman raised her arm and placed her wrist near Jario's mouth. Lara turned her head not wanting to watch him or see the blood upon his lips.

"See Lara," he said, as Lara tuned back toward Jario. "She offers her wrist to me. I am not harming her."

He opened his mouth and extended his fangs before he bit into the flesh of her wrist. He felt the warm blood wash against the inside of his mouth and down his throat. Closing his eyes, he drank for only a moment and then licked her wrist to stop the blood flow. Bringing her back to the cot, he took the woman's wrist and held it to Lara's mouth.

"Drink," he ordered. "The need you feel will only get worse. Drink or you will die of hunger."

Lara pulled away, as far as her restraints would allow. She turned her head, refusing to drink from the woman.

"You know your hunger will get worse," he reminded her. "The madness also comes when hunger is not fed and that madness is worse. It brings an evil that is almost impossible to return from. It seizes complete control of you."

Lara felt her body tremble as Jario walked back to the table dragging the young woman by her arm. Unfortunately, she knew he was right. Avoiding the hunger was worse, but she had to hold out as long as she could.

Pulling the bread from the basket and ripping off a hunk, he handed it to the woman. She ate it quickly and reached for more.

Jario slapped her hand away from the basket and scolded, "This small ration has to last you a few days, my dear."

She sat back and folded her hands in her lap.

"Rest a while. I plan on playing a few games later this evening."

The woman's eyes closed and she slumped over resting her arms against the wooden table to support her head.

Walking out the door to calm his frustration, he decided he

should scout the area for any signs of the Evergreen Army. Scanning the cottage, he found it was well hidden by fallen trees and dry shrubs. From a distance, it looked like nothing more than a pile of stones. Not needing the heat of a fire, there would be no smoke to smell or track to the location. The only light was from the few candles he used in the cottage, but they were so dim it would appear to be nothing more than the moon reflecting on the rocks. Comfortable with his hiding place, he roamed about the surrounding area. The stone cottage was several miles beyond the entrance to the canyon. Even if the army entered the canyon, they would have to decide which direction to search.

What if they headed in their direction, he thought? How long would it take them to find the cottage without vampire powers? They would be searching every cave along the way.

Speeding toward the entrance using his haze, he could hear the army off in the distance making their way down the cliffs. He realized they had figured out where he had gone sooner than he thought they would. Watching the unit head in the opposite direction, he felt secure in his hiding place for the night. They would have to search both sides of the canyon before turning around and heading in his direction.

Arriving back at the cottage, he circled around listening for any sounds coming from inside. Hearing none, he sped beyond the cottage in search of a place much further into the canyon that would be better hidden from view. If he found something, he would move Lara and the woman tomorrow night allowing more distance between the army and his future mate. He needed the time to allure her toward the human blood and eventually his own. The time remaining that allowed him to use his powers within the canyon was running out. Knowing the army was in the canyon searching for him, he had to make progress, risk capture, or worse.

After running for several miles, he spotted a dark area behind several large boulders. He had almost missed it. Catching the reflection of the moon at just the right moment had allowed him to see the indentation in the side of the cliff. The opening was small and would be missed easily in the dark by vampires without their powers. He approached the opening and ducked inside. He had to crawl about ten feet before he was able to stand inside an area that was three times his height wide and that again long. The ground was dry, and there wasn't any moisture on the walls. He had found a perfect place to hide. Crawling back out into the night air, he sped back toward the cottage.

It is about time I had some fun for a change, he thought, as he felt the cool breeze brush against his face. Tonight could be interesting.

Chapter 23

Feeling the rope burn blisters within the palms of his hands, Tate kept moving down toward the bottom of the canyon. Several of the men had already made their way to the bottom and had started assembling their groups to start searching. As his feet hit the floor of the canyon, he looked about in the darkness. His vision was no longer that of a vampire, and he already felt the weakness in his body from his loss of powers and the climb down the cliffs. Looking up, he watched as more men made their way down the cliff wall and knew that Thomas would be the last to take to the ropes.

Realizing, he had to make a choice between going east or west, he worried that his choice would lead him in the wrong direction. If he split the army into two units to travel in both directions like he had planned, he risked not having enough men to capture Jario. He had to choose and quickly.

"We'll head east," Tate shouted. "We'll go no more than ten miles, and if we find nothing, we'll turn back and search the other direction."

Several men wanted to split the unit in half and search both directions hoping to save time, but he had to explain his reasoning for staying together.

Frances, the last man down, joined the group. Tate looked back at the cliffs and didn't see Thomas anywhere. He asked Frances, "Was Thomas on the rope heading down?" He worried for his brother now that he was without sight. If he fell, it could be the end of him or worse.

"He was still standing at the cliff's edge when I was half way down. I felt the rope shake when he started to descend, but he is moving really slow."

"We can't wait for him," Tate said. "Let's get moving. We are chasing Jario, and the sun will be upon us soon enough. We'll need to find some kind of shelter before some of us fry in the morning light." After hiding the gear they used on the cliffs, they secured their weapons and headed east in search of Jario and Lady Lara.

* * *

Thomas was starting to regret his willingness to descend the cliffs. Inching slowly hand over hand, he made his way down toward the bottom of the canyon feeling his skin burn from the blisters rubbing against the coarse rope. The pain caused him to stop frequently and rest. He had listened to the men shout as they gave instructions for controlling their bodies and how to carefully hold the rope. Trying to apply their words into actions proved to be grueling work. The new challenge of his blindness made it difficult to avoid the sharp rocks that jutted from the side of the cliff and scraped his back and shoulders. The voices of the men once heard easily were now faint, and he knew they had moved on without him. He was on his own and only had himself to blame for the huge mistake that caused him the loss of his eyesight.

Finally feeling the ground under his feet, he sighed in relief to have made it without falling. His hands were raw, and he could feel wetness on his shoulder that meant he was bleeding. Brushing his hair from his eyes, he felt a long scrape on his forehead that had crusted over with dry blood. Looking about as if he could see which direction to proceed, he saw nothing but complete darkness. Moving back until he felt his body hit the side of the cliff, he listened and determined the men had moved in an easterly direction.

Since I am by myself, I may as well head the other way, he thought.

Stepping away from the cliff, he took a deep breath and said out loud, as if someone was listening, "Wispets! If you can hear me, I could use some extra powers. I'm grateful for what you have given me, but they don't seem to work down in this canyon. Whatever you can provide would be appreciated to help me find Lady Lara, the lady that I love."

He laughed to himself as he stepped away from the cliff a good ten paces and turned west. He hoped he was not heading toward his death.

Stumbling through dead tree branches and tripping over rocks, Thomas made his way through the canyon floor. It wasn't long before he realized he had no idea what he was looking for. He was spending more time trying to keep himself from falling than searching for Lara.

Finding a boulder near his feet, he sat down to rest and figure out how to approach the search, as a blind man. Resting, he began to listen to the wind. It moved about the canyon bouncing against things that were in its way. He could hear the rustle of tree branches above him and shrubs at his feet. Sniffing the air, the rotting tree bark filled his nostrils. He knew the sweet scent of Lara, and if he was near her, he would smell the lemon and mint that she loved so much. Bending down and touching some branches that had fallen from a tree, he ran his hand against the rough bark feeling the broken tips of the branch. The branch was broken away from him as if someone had walked through the branch snapping it from the pressure of someone's leg.

Could this be the path that Jario took through the canyon, he thought, filling his mind with hope.

Suddenly, the realization that he had his senses to help him search for Lara gave him all the encouragement he needed. He knew she was within his grasp.

Bending slightly and letting his hand brush against the dried remains of the canyon, Thomas followed the broken twigs and trampled shrubs that seemed to give the impression of a path that had been used recently. Occasionally, he stood and listened to the wind hoping to hear a voice and inhaled the air searching for her lovely scent. His progress was slow, but he was determined to stay the course.

Remembering that his powers had been lost, he became distressed about how much darkness was left before the sun would rise. He would no longer be able to walk in the daylight and needed to find shelter. He tried to figure out how much time had passed, but not seeing the moon hindered his result. His only hope for survival was to find a small cave that was deep enough to hide him from the sun. Turning in the direction he believed to be the side of the cliff, he counted his steps to remember how far the path was from the cliff. He stretched out his arms stepping carefully until his hands touched the rough rock counting thirty-five paces.

Following the cliff, he listened to the wind and for a change in its direction. Not noticing a change in the wind's patterns but a hollow howling sound, he kept moving forward. The howling sound got louder and louder with each step. He could feel the wind disappear from around his legs and then burst out against them. He had found an opening in the canyon wall. Crouching down, Thomas felt about the edges of the opening. Reaching in, his hand waved about finding nothing but air. He crawled into the space holding his hand out in front of him as he went. After what he thought was about fifteen feet, he stopped and attempted to sit. Not feeling the rocks scraping against his head, he knew there was room for him to sit comfortably and wait until the darkness came again. It was then that the thought of Lara consumed him and brought him to tears. He feared for her safety and wanted nothing more than to hold her in his arms. He thought of the few times he had kissed her gently and felt her return the tenderness. Attempting to pull his vision in search of Lara, he reached as deep as he could to hunt for her. His vision offered nothing but darkness. He wondered if his visions were full of darkness because he was blind or because he had lost his power. The need to continue searching the canyon made him want to leave the cave, but he feared the sun. The thought of the sun rising calmed his need to continue searching and made him wait for the darkness to come again. Resting his back against the wall of the cave, he whispered out load to the Wispets, "If you can't help me, please help Lara."

Feeling good about his plan to move the women to the cave further into the canyon, Jario was smiling as he entered the stone cottage. The woman was still sleeping and Lara sat on the cot leaning against the wall with her knees pulled against her chest. The idea of spreading her knees and taking her as his mate, heightened his desire for her. Heading in her direction, he could see her tighten her grasp around her knees, and her face was filled with anger. Jario sat down on the cot next to her and pulled her hand into his. She struggled to pull it away, but he kept it firmly in his grasp moving his fingers in a circle over her tiny wrist. He bent to kiss her open hand, but she closed it realizing what he intended to do. Furious, he threw her hand back at her and walked over to the sleeping woman. Circling the table and watching the woman sleep, he felt his fury build from the refusal Lara had shown him.

"Wake," he shouted, as she sat up looking about the room. "Follow me."

Stepping to the middle of the room, Jario watched as she followed him standing directly in front of him.

"Undress yourself slowly," he smirked, as he looked in Lara's direction.

Jario watched as the woman released the few pieces of clothing she wore. Standing naked in front of him, he walked around her studying her plump breasts and dark curls that rested below her belly. He ran his hand down her back feeling the curves of her bottom. He took the dagger from his boot and handed it to the woman.

"No!" Lara screamed and jerked her hands trying to release the rope. "I order you to stop. Do not hurt her."

Jario stepped in Lara's direction looking down into her eyes as he smirked, "You order me? You no longer order me, Lara." He saw her eyes fill with fear for the woman and herself. "What will you give me to stop?"

Fearing she had played right into his hands, she cringed as she spoke, "You wanted to kiss my hand. Here, I will allow you to kiss my hand."

Jario laughed and stepped directly in front of Lara looking down at her outstretched hand. He knocked it away with his knee as he replied, "The price has gone up since your refusal. I would prefer to kiss your lovely bare neck."

She froze remembering the way he scraped his fangs against her skin and tasted her blood. Fearing what he would make the woman do, she sat up and pulled her unraveling braid from her neck. She sat quietly offering him the price he requested to keep the woman safe.

Jario licked his lips and sat down next to Lara pulling her into his body. He could feel the softness of her breast against his chest and indulged his senses as he inhaled her sweet scent. Leaning toward her neck, he slipped his tongue from his mouth and swept it across her shoulder and up her neck to her ear. His eyes rolled back as he felt the lust of hunger rise within him. Gently he kissed her neck, and she felt his fangs drag against her skin. The instant her blood hit his tongue, his mouth burst with excitement, and his arousal flared. He sat consumed with the intimate feeling and wanted to explore every bit of her. Feeling her pull from his arms, he sat back and looked hopefully into her eyes. She returned nothing but the look of disgust. He forcefully pushed her back and stood. Glaring down at her, he turned and walked back to the woman he had left standing naked in the middle of the room.

Standing before the woman, he paced back and forth in front of her and then grabbed the dagger from her hands. Shoving it back into his boot, he ordered, "Cover yourself and prepare to sleep on the floor." Following his instructions, she was soon sleeping soundly.

Leaving the woman on the floor, Jario stepped toward the cot and watched Lara turn her body toward the wall. He stripped off his clothes and sat down on the edge of the cot leaning against her back.

"You have not fed," he said. "You can't go much longer without feeding. If you will not take blood from this woman, you need to take it from me."

She shook her head and pulled closer to the wall. He curled his body around her back and could feel her body quiver. Pulling her braid to the side exposing her neck, he ran his fingers from her ear to her shoulder. He had loved her once, but she had made it clear that she would not return his affection. Leaving that thought of rejection behind, he closed his eyes and thought of his future power as Evergreen's master until he drifted off to sleep.

Lara felt his fingers touch her neck and finally the feel of his relaxed body as he slept. She reached her fingers under the mattress of the cot and felt for the hinge. It was still secure in place. She would only have one chance to use it against Jario. If she failed, he would surely take what he wanted without hesitation. She had to make her move soon. Since she still had not taken blood, the madness would start to come to her quickly. She was already feeling the hunger and watching Jario bite the woman's wrist made her thirst raise the dreaded desire. Soon rational thinking would leave her, and the madness would seize hold of her without being able to stop it. She could only hope that Thomas and the army would find her before that happened.

* * *

Making their way through the canyon floor, Tate and the rest of the army fought through the thick dry shrubbery full of thorns that stung when they met their flesh. The darkness made it difficult to see much beyond their own outstretched arm and kept the searching at a slow pace. They had searched every cave or small stone cottage that had been abandoned by the Wispets, finding nothing that would indicate that Jario had been anywhere near this end of the canyon. The sky was beginning to lighten, and the need for shelter was becoming urgent.

Tate called several of the men together to discuss their options. Continuing too much longer would put them at risk with the sun steadily approaching. Shelter was needed and soon. They could continue on in hopes of finding a cave or cottage to spend the daylight hours or turn back to the places they had passed along the way.

"We have not found any trail to follow," said Tate. "The sun comes soon, and we need to shelter. What say you? Do we continue in the direction we have been searching? Or, do we turn back to take shelter and then search the other direction when darkness comes again?"

The men talked among themselves as they weighed their options. The humans offered to continue searching beyond where they stood. Daylight would make the search easier, and they could cover the few remaining miles much quicker. If Jario was discovered in hiding, they could storm the location and force him into the sunlight. If they found nothing, they would circle back and join the command to start searching the other end of the canyon. It was decided that the humans could search the additional miles and return back to report their findings. If nothing was found, the return of darkness would direct the search in the opposite direction.

Making their way back to a cave they had passed during the search, the army separated into two groups. The vampires began to enter the cave and wait for darkness, as the humans continued on in hopes of finding Lady Lara alone. Tate watched as the small command of humans left to search the remaining distance. Satisfied that they were doing all they could, he turned and ducked down to enter the narrow opening.

Reaching the back of the cave, he leaned against the wall and spoke to the command, "We have done the best we could tonight. Get some rest. When evening comes, we will begin our search of the other end of the canyon. Jario has to be hiding in this canyon. We will find him and bring our Lady to safety."

Trying to sleep, Tate closed his eyes but saw nothing but his brother wandering alone in the canyon and feared for his safety. Knowing the sun was rising, he worried that Thomas would not realize he needed to take shelter, and he would be found burned among the rocks of the canyon. He had hoped that Thomas would have stayed at the entrance and not made his way down the ropes, but he understood his need to find Lady Lara. He hoped they would find where Jario was hiding and either stake him or find a way to arrest him.

Chapter 24

Hearing the heavy wind, Jario woke and sat up on the side of the cot. He walked to the door and opened it stepping outside in the darkness. A storm was coming, and he could feel the signs of it in the air. He could already see debris from the canyon floor being picked up by the wind as it swirled around him. The coming weather would surely slow the army in their search and give him more of the time he needed to reach his goal. The sooner he got the women moved to the cave, the more protected he would be from capture. He walked back into the cottage and knelt down next to the woman he had left on the floor.

"Wake," he said. "Stand and follow me."

She stood and followed Jario out the door into the darkness. He took her wrist and bit down drawing the red liquid from her veins. He swallowed her blood feeling the need to drain her, but he knew he would need her later and stopped as he felt her sway. Wiping his lips with his tongue, he dropped her arm to her side. He ran his hand down between her breasts. Cupping one within his hand, he sank his fangs into its flesh and drew until blood filled his mouth. He ripped her flesh as he pulled his fangs back from her breast. Swallowing the rich liquid, he felt his arousal start to stir within him. Pulling her into his body, he sank his fangs into her neck and drew in more blood. Avoiding his need to find release, he pushed her toward the door of the cottage.

"Go in and sit at the table. You need to eat," he said, as he followed her back into the cottage.

He pulled the bread and cheese from the basket and sat a small portion of each on the table in front of her. Walking toward his clothes, he watched Lara as she moved slightly. He stared at her neck as he bent to reach for his breeches. The taste of her sweet blood was intoxicating, and he was sure it would not be much longer before she gave it to him willingly. He knew he could use the woman against Lara and get what he wanted. If not tonight, it would happen tomorrow.

Time was running out. Once he finished dressing, he walked back over to the woman.

"Come with me," he said.

She followed him through the door. Without telling Lara what he was doing, he threw the woman over his shoulder and sped toward the cave he had found further into the canyon. The wind was getting worse, and it clouded his visibility within the canyon. Slowing, he hunted for the entrance to the cave. Finally finding it, Jario ordered the woman to crawl into the cave as he followed her. Once inside he ordered her to sit against the wall and not move. Leaving her there, he left the cave and raced back to the cottage to retrieve Lara.

Entering the cottage, he found Lara awake and sitting with both feet on the floor. Jario walked over to Lara and reached for his dagger. He bent down and cut the ropes that had secured her to the bed. Lara lifted her hands toward Jario and pushed his chest away from her as far as she could. Reaching for the metal hinge, she pulled it from the cot's webbing. Before she could strike, he gripped her wrist tightly and twisted it until the hinge fell from her hand.

"You foolish woman," Jario snarled. "You think to harm me?" He felt her try to pull her wrist from his grasp. "You are going to hurt yourself. Keep this up and you will feel my fangs in your throat." Her movements stilled and tears fell from her eyes. "We are moving," he said, as he kicked the hinge across the floor.

Lara pulled back trying to put distance between them. He grabbed her other arm and picked her up throwing her over his shoulder. Before stepping through the cottage, he snatched the remaining candles and the basket with the remains of the bread and cheese. The wind howled and blew dirt and dead branches back and forth across the canyon. He stopped several times to pull debris that had twisted around his legs before he arrived at the entrance to the cave.

Once inside, he sat Lara down next to the woman and stood brushing dirt from his face and hair. Pulling a candle from the basket, he soon had a dim glow about the small dry cavern. Removing his tunic, he used it to wipe his face and shoulders. Shaking his tunic to remove the dirt, he then stooped down to wipe the dirt from Lara's face. She sat still as she let him remove the twigs that had become tangled in her hair. Looking to her right, she could see the woman that was now sitting right next to her. Being this close, she could hear her heartbeat and tried to ignore it. The smell of the blood that lingered on her body caused Lara to inhale deeply. She moved slightly away from the woman and looked in the opposite direction. Jario noticed her movement and knew exactly what was happening. Lara's need for blood was getting worse.

"You need to feed," he said. "You can't wait much longer."

Lara shook her head and closed her eyes.

"There are no animals in this dead canyon," he said, as he attempted to reason with her. "You have a choice. Drink from me or the woman."

Lara looked up at Jario and said, "Please don't make me drink her blood."

Jario bent down in front of Lara and pulled his dagger from his boot. He cut his wrist and forced it to her mouth. She pulled back keeping her mouth tightly closed. The smell of his blood slowly took control of her senses, and she could control herself no longer. She latched her mouth upon the open wound and drank. Jario reeled with the sensation of feeling her draw his blood. It was the most intimate feeling he had ever felt. As he reached to pull her toward him, she released her mouth from his wrist and pushed his arm away.

"That is all. No more!" she said, as she gasped trying to control her breathing. She wiped her mouth with the hem of her skirt and turned her head away from him and the woman sitting beside her.

"You will need more," he responded. "Tell me if you need more."

She shook her head and raised the back of her hand to cover her eyes, willing away her need for more blood. Agitated, he stood and reached for the woman sitting next to Lara. Pulling her against his chest, he bit into her neck and drew her blood into his mouth. Not feeling the satisfaction he had hoped for from the woman, he dropped her back to the floor of the cavern. He paced the width of the small space feeling his frustration building and the desire for Lara's blood steadily increasing.

"I will not wait much longer," he shouted at Lara. "I will have you before the night is over."

Exiting the cave, he felt the wind swirl around his body and the need to relieve his frustration and anger. His time was running out. Jario needed to mate with Lara and find a way back to the castle without a surprise encounter from the army that searched for him. Pulling his haze, he sped off in the direction he had last seen the army. Knowing there was a small contingent of humans that could search in the sunlight made him anxious that they may have found his trail.

Off in the distance, he could hear the sounds of a great many men shouting, he knew he was close to the army. They had gone the other direction to search and were now just starting to head back toward the entrance to the canyon, where they had started. The army would be heading in his direction and searching every place that could be used for hiding. He wouldn't be able to retrieve Lara, reach the entrance and climb the cliff without being seen. He had not planned his exit of the canyon and was now left to find another way out. The exit needed to be closer to the cave, and he needed to fine one quickly.

Heading back in the direction of the cave, he ran in a back and forth pattern to disguise his trail and hoping the wind would assist in covering of his footprints. As he reached the outside of the cave, he stopped to listen for any sounds coming from inside the hollow space. They were quiet, but he could hear the heartbeat of the woman and the sound of Lara's feet as she nervously tapped the cavern floor. He knew she was trying to control her hunger. He would finally mate with her tonight before leaving the canyon and solve both of their problems, her need for blood and his need for power.

Jario sped to the other side of the canyon. He walked slowly examining the cliff for any path that might allow him to easily climb with Lara over his shoulder or would allow her to climb with his assistance. He walked for about a mile before he found a section of the canyon wall that appeared to have enough gouges to allow his hands and feet to pull himself up and out of the canyon. Making his way up the crags of the canyon wall, he stepped carefully from jagged rock to the few indentations left where a rock had come loose and fallen. The path was treacherous. If he stepped carefully, he felt he could make the climb without a great degree of difficulty. Finally reaching the top and pulling himself out of the canyon, he sighed with relief. He had found a way out of the canyon. All that was left to do now was mating with Lara and returning to the castle as the new master.

Jario bent over examining the cliffs edge. The canyon wall was not a straight drop, and he decided he wouldn't be able to drop over the edge like he did at the entrance. He would have to climb back down. Turning and kneeling at the edge, he reached back with a foot to gain a secure foothold on a rock. Slowly, he made his way down the cliff. The wind that had bothered him earlier had now been replaced with a light rain. Careful to have secure footing on the slippery rocks, he slowed his pace. Reaching for a root that had benefited him on the way up, his foot slipped, and he lost his balance for a moment. Regaining his stability, he leaned again as he reached for the root. Feeling it securely in his hand, he pulled his body over to make contact with the next jagged rock. Before his foot was secure, the root released itself from the side of the cliff, and Jario plummeted backward. As he fell, he tried to grab anything that was within his reach. His back slammed against jagged rocks, and he felt the sting of thorns scrape against his face. The canyon floor received his body as he slammed into it. Feeling a sharp throbbing pain, he reached for his shoulder. He felt the end of a broken branch that had impaled his neck and broken his shoulder. Blood gushed from the wound, as he tried to remove himself from the twisted branch. More and more blood streamed from his body. Struggling to remove the branch, his grip slipped from the blood that covered his hands. Jario looked up at the stars feeling his vision blur. He slowly watched as the stars dimmed, and the darkness took him.

* * *

Crawling toward the opening of the small cave, Thomas inhaled the air trying to determine if darkness had fallen. He could hear the sound of the howling wind as it swirled around the canyon and was struck a number of times by bits of debris that had been hurled through the entrance. Bravely he stuck his arm out into the open air, as he waited for the pain of burning flesh. Pulling his arm back unharmed, he let a sigh of relief escape him, as he exited into the night air.

Squaring his shoulders to the wall of rock behind him, he counted his steps to try and regain any trail that may still be undamaged from the wind. Squatting, he felt the ground with his hands as he desperately searched for a sign that would lead him to Lara. Not finding anything obvious, he stood and started walking as he carefully listened to the wind. He could feel the coming rain and dreaded the mud that would hinder his search even more.

He thought he was making pretty good progress for being blind. He had found a long smooth branch that he was able to hold out in front of him to detect the frequent rocks that he had been tripping over earlier. Noticing a change in the wind patterns, Thomas felt something larger than the usual boulder was in his path. He carefully approached the object finding several large boulders and stacks of smaller rocks that appeared to be some kind of wall. He walked around the object feeling with his hands until his fingers touched the broken pains of a window.

This was probably one of the cottages that belonged to the Wispets, he thought, as he tripped over something and nearly fell.

Reaching out with both hands, he felt the fur of an animal. Being a farmer, he knew right away it was a goat and could feel that its neck had been cut. Someone had killed the goat for its blood and that someone had to be Jario. He was on the right path. He made his way to the door of the cottage and listened carefully for any sounds coming from inside. Not hearing anything, he pushed the door the rest of the way open and was immediately greeted with the sweet scent of lemon and mint. Lara had been in the cottage, and he was getting closer. He wondered why they had left the security of the cottage, and he surmised that Jario knew the army was searching the canyon. He had probably moved to a location further away. Not wasting any time, he left the cottage stopping every now and then to inhale the air in hopes of picking up her sweet scent.

A light rain began to fall, and he could hear the water that had collected in the dry riverbed start to move along the rocks. Not finding anymore cottages in his path, he determined that Jario would have taken shelter within a cave just as he had done. The question before him was which side of the canyon to search. He had been lucky, so far, and hoped his luck would continue as he headed for the right side of the canyon. The wall of rocks were sharp under his hands. The wall of the canyon afforded him the ease of a straight path along its edge and very few boulders to climb over. He felt like he had walked for hours and his body was telling him he needed to rest. Ignoring his fatigue, he kept moving forward and listening for any sounds that would indicate Jario was near.

Coming to a cluster of a few small and several large boulders, he walked between them and the wall of the canyon feeling the rocks as he went. With his next step, his hand felt nothing but air. He had found a cave. Checking to make sure his dagger was secure in his boot, he bent down and started to crawl slowly through a tunnel. Listening for any sound that would warn him of danger, he crept further into the tunnel. The walls were dry, and the dirt beneath his hands were full of deep ridges. The ridges were wide and long, as if someone had crawled in and used this cave for shelter. He slowed for fear that Jario would be waiting for him as he entered the cave. Feeling a small rock beneath his hand, he picked it up and threw it forward listening for any sudden movement. Hearing none, he moved forward and then stopped as he caught the scent of something familiar.

A soft voice spoke, "Who is there?"

Recognizing the voice, Thomas moved as quickly as he could until he reached the inside of the cave.

"Thomas," Lara cried. "My love, you found me. I never gave up. I knew you would search for me."

He stood cautiously, reaching his arms over his head to assure he could stand and then stretched his arms out toward her voice and asked, "Lara my love, are you well? Did he hurt you? I need you to come to me. I need to feel that you are well."

Lara stood and reached her arms around him pulling his body tightly against hers. "I knew you would come for me. Have you brought the army?" Lara looked up at Thomas and saw the dirt and dried blood that stuck to the stubble upon his face. "Jario has not been gone long. We must leave quickly," she said. "Jario could return at any moment." Remembering the woman that shared the cave, she glanced over her shoulder. "There is a young woman with me, and we need to take her with us."

Releasing Thomas for a moment, she reached for the woman's arm and helped her stand. Taking her hand, she pulled her toward Thomas.

"Follow me out of the cave," he said. "We have a great distance to travel before we are back to the entrance of the canyon, and Jario will surely follow us once he discovers you are gone."

Thomas led them out of the cave and into the night air. With his arms out in front of him, he tried to reach for her. Not immediately finding her, he hunted for her by moving his arms.

"Thomas, what is wrong?" Lara asked. "What has happened?"

He bent his head down and uttered, "I have lost my sight."

Rushing to him, Lara ran her hand over his eyes looking for any sign of a wound. She stood on tiptoes and kissed his chin. Feeling his arms wrap around her, she pressed her face to his chest, "Who hurt you, Thomas?"

"I will tell you what happened once we are out of danger," he said. "For now, we need to hurry. Jario could return at any moment. We are not safe here."

"Thomas, take my arm," said Lara. "I will be your eyes."

Lara gave her arm to Thomas and with the other arm she reached for the young woman. Taking her by the hand, they began their journey back to the entrance of the canyon.

* * *

The army was spread across the canyon floor as they searched for any sign of Jario or Thomas. Tate worried that they would find him dead among the boulders either from falling or from Jario's blade. Since they didn't have to spend time searching beyond their cave, they had made good time back to the point where they had entered the canyon. The wind that had slowed them down had finally stopped, and the light rain seemed to take the tiredness from their bodies.

"I see a cottage up ahead," shouted Will, as he pointed toward the cluster of stacked stones.

Carefully approaching the stone structure, several members of the command circled the building.

"Someone's been here recently," whispered Frances. "There is a dead goat, and the blood has been drained from its neck."

Finding the door open, Tate slowly entered with his dagger ready to strike. Looking around the small space, he could tell it had been occupied recently. Moving toward the cot, he saw the remains of rope that had been cut with a blade and dark dry droplets of blood on the stone floor.

Seeing the cottage was empty, he yelled, "They were here, but they have gone!"

They quickly moved around the cottage and continued on through the canyon. Shortly after leaving the empty cottage, Frances stopped abruptly. Waving his arms to get attention, he pointed off in the distance. Seeing the men look his way, he held up his hand showing three fingers indicating he had seen three figures. Tate scanned the area and could see dark figures walking closely together. Signaling for the command to circle around the trio, they prepared for the possibility of an attack from Jario.

Once everyone was in place, Frances shouted, "Stop where you are!"

Continuing to move forward, Thomas replied, as loud as he could, "We need to keep moving! Lady Lara is in danger."

Hearing the familiar voice, Tate ran to meet the trio followed by Frances. Taking Lady Lara's hand from Thomas, Frances led her and the young woman to the protection of a command that immediately surrounded them. Tate grabbed his brother and hugged him tightly.

"I thought I had lost you," he said, as he took Thomas by the arm and led him back to the awaiting army. "Head to the entrance as quickly as possible," ordered Tate. "We need to get out of this damn canyon and back to Evergreen."

Chapter 25

Lara was grateful the army had returned unharmed. They had been brave to enter the Canyon of Obscurity, knowing their powers would be useless against Jario. Yet, they risked their own lives to search for her and ultimately saved Thomas and the young woman, as well as, herself. She owed them a debt that she would never be able to repay.

Lara had made sure the young woman that had been held with her was put in Flora's care. Feeling the need to check on the woman, she made her way to the Healing Room. She was surprised to find Tate sitting by the bed of another woman. Tate looked up and stood as Lady Lara entered the room.

"Please sit," Lara whispered. Peering over his shoulder, she looked at the woman's bruised and battered face. "Tate, who is this?"

"Her name is Gavenia," answered Tate. He lifted her hand and stroked her long fingers with his own. "She is the woman that was held with me at Black Thistle Castle. She had been severely tortured by Magna and was almost dead when I found her. I brought her back to Evergreen the evening you were taken. My Lady, she has been asleep ever since she arrived, and I fear that she will never wake."

Lara stepped around the foot of the cot and placed a hand upon Tate's shoulder to try and give him some comfort.

"She will wake once she is healed. It often takes the mind longer than the body to heal," she said softly. "She is in good care. I am sure Flora will do her best to help her. Be patient, she sleeps to keep from feeling the pain."

Tate nodded and continued to stroke Gavenia's hand. He felt helpless. He wanted to take the pain away from her. He wanted to hold her and tell her he was sorry for his part in her suffering.

Stepping over to the other cot, Lara saw the young woman that was held by Jario was awake. She sat down on the edge of the bed and took the woman's hand.

"My name is Lara," she said. "You are in Evergreen Castle and have nothing to fear from anyone here. What is your name?"

The woman pushed herself up to lean against the wooden frame of the cot as she spoke, "My name is Niobe. It means Fern, but I think Niobe is prettier."

Smiling, Lara gently squeezed Niobe's hand as she replied, "It is a lovely name." Seeing the patches of cloth that covered her wounds, she watched Niobe bring her hand up to her neck and then close her eyes. "Do your wounds cause you any pain?"

"They hurt when I move," Niobe replied. "How did I get them? I do not remember anything after climbing down the canyon wall."

"It is best you do not remember," Lara said, as she stroked the side of Niobe's face. "They were caused by the desires of a traitor for power. The army has been charged with arresting him. Once found, he will be sentenced to a final death for his crimes." Lara could see the fear in Niobe's eyes and regretted her words. "I am sorry I upset you. Let's speak of something else. Where is your home?"

"My home is near Whistler's River in a small village called Wintergreen Mountain. The men folk there cut down trees to build log cottages," she explained. "They also send the logs down the river toward Old Mill to be cut. After they are cut, they travel down Wood Cutter's Water to Wood's Bay. Once there, they are sold and carried away by the ships. The fallen trees have a very long journey to make before the men receive their coin in payment, but when they do, they spend the money at the tavern."

"Do you wish to return to your home?" Lara asked. "If you do, I will have a member of the army escort you safely home."

Niobe closed her eyes and bent her head downward, clasping her hands as she shook her head and replied, "I have no family in the village. I worked at the tavern and lived in a small room above the kitchen. If you will allow me, I would like to stay here. I am willing to work for my keep."

Lara patted Niobe's hands and smiled as she replied, "You may stay if you like. We can talk about other things once you are well."

Seeing her smile, Lara stood and bid Niobe and Tate good evening. She had someone else to visit.

* * *

The hallways of the castle were buzzing with the news of the safe return of Lady Lara. A celebration was being planned for the following evening and everyone was busy preparing food, drink and music for dancing. Servants moved about the hallways carrying supplies to the

Great Hall. The sounds of laughter once again filled the castle.

Making her way through the crowded hallways to his chamber door, Lara thought about how lucky she was to have found Thomas. He showed courage in the midst of every barrier that presented itself. Thomas was her champion, and she loved him above all others. He was blind, but his blindness would not get in the way of their love. It was a challenge and nothing more.

Hearing a knock at the door, McDuff pulled the large wooden door open to find Lady Lara smiling back at him. Grinning from ear to ear, McDuff bowed slightly as Lara entered the room. Seeing Thomas sitting by the fire, she quietly approached his chair and knelt down in front of him. Taking his hands, she once again felt the special sensation they shared race through her body.

"I have missed you," she whispered before kissing the palms of his hands. She was glad to see that the raw blisters from descending down the ropes had finally healed.

He leaned forward inhaling her scent of lemon and mint giving his body a feeling of peace. Lifting his hand, he searched for her face. She took his hand and placed it upon her cheek.

"I will miss seeing your lovely face," he said, as his eyes filled with tears. "I will never be able to see your beauty again."

She stood slowly, stepping between his knees and sitting on his lap. Wrapping her arms around his shoulders, she spoke softly in his ear, "I am beautiful because you make me feel beautiful." Seeing a single tear fall from his eye, Lara kissed his forehead and then turned his face with her hand. "I love you, Thomas." She softly kissed each of his lifeless eyes.

Feeling her tender touch, he placed his arm around her waist. Pulling her body tightly against his own, he filled his mind with a picture of her angelic face. They held each other enjoying the simple touch of their bodies and the love they shared for one another.

McDuff made a coughing sound to interrupt the couple. "My Lady," he spoke, as he stood at attention beside the door. "Charlotte has dinner ready for you in your private courtyard. Should I have her serve you in your chamber?"

"McDuff, we will eat in the courtyard," Lara replied. "It will be good for us to sit under the stars."

They reluctantly released each other, and Lara took hold of Thomas' hand and brought it lovingly to her lips. Kissing his fingers, she watched as a smile was finally present upon his face.

"It is nice to see you smile," she said, as she tucked his arm through her own and led him toward the door.

* * *

Seated at the table, Thomas was frustrated after knocking over his cup for the second time.

"I have an idea," Lara said, as she touched his hand assuredly. "Have you tried your vision gift since you left the canyon? There is nothing here that would restrict your gifted powers."

He had forgotten about the gift since his unsuccessful attempts in the canyon. Pulling the vision to his present location, a light blurry fog began to appear. The edges were dark, and he feared he had also lost the gift along with his eyesight. He concentrated on bringing the scene into focus, the fog began to disappear and before him, sat Lara.

"I can see your beautiful face," he cried. "Thank the heavens, I can see you."

He struggled, but he managed to hold the vision throughout dinner. Seeing his vision begin to blur, he felt his energy failing and soon her image was gone.

"It was wonderful while it lasted," he sighed. "I am too weak to hold it any longer."

They walked arm in arm about the courtyard enjoying the cool breeze and the sweet scent of the night blooming flowers by the fountain. Lara described the way the moon and stars brightened the night sky. They spoke of his visit to see Velsa and her fear of Jario. Each word they spoke lessened the darkness that had seized them both.

Lara watched the sky as it began to lighten. "We must go in," Lara said, as she tried to lead Thomas toward the door. "The sun is beginning to rise. I must return you to your chamber."

He stalled and nervously took her by the shoulders as he asked, "Is it too much of a burden to love a blind man? Do you fear that I will not be able to protect you or anyone in the castle?" He dreaded the response that she would offer.

Lara reached her arms around him placing her face against his chest and feeling his arms encircle her body. Enjoying the closeness of his body she replied, "You will never be a burden to me, my love. You are everything to me."

Determined to see her once more, he struggled to pull his vision. Seeing her lovely face before him, he knelt before her and looked up into her eyes.

"My beautiful Lara," he said, as he felt his voice catch in his throat from nerves. "I love you above all others. Will you do me the honor of becoming my mate for all eternity?"

Tears began to fill Lara's eyes as she knelt before him. Placing her hands on either side of his face, she looked directly into his eyes and said, "Thomas, I love you above all others. I will be honored to become your mate for all eternity."

With a sigh of relief, he reached into his leather vest pocket. He retrieved an intricate gold ring with a center stone the color of her blue eyes and a sprinkling of tiny emeralds surrounding the center stone. Placing it upon her finger, he kissed the back of her hand as he had the first night they dined in the courtyard.

"It is beautiful, my love," she whispered, in his ear. Embracing him, she was happier than she had ever been. "Thomas, it is as beautiful as your love for me."

They held each other, looking up at the last of the stars in the evening sky and the beginning of a new day. It would be their beginning to share for all eternity.

"Now, we can go inside," he said, with utter joy in his voice.

* * *

Opening his eyes and feeling the sharp pain in his neck and shoulder, Jario remembered slamming into the floor of the canyon. Carefully he pushed his body into a sitting position. The blood had stopped running from his shoulder, and the wound had started to heal around the embedded branch. He was covered in rocks and debris that had fallen from the rocky wall to the canyon floor.

The storm must have gotten worse after my fall, he thought, as he tried to push the branches, dirt and rocks from his mangled body. Had it not been for the storm, I would have surely turned to ash in the sun.

He noticed the dim morning light and knew he needed to quickly return to the cave for shelter. Worry for Lara filled his thoughts. She would be in need of blood by now. He had left her alone with the woman and knew her resolve would be weakened. In this weakened state, it would be time to take her as his own.

He stood and leaned against the canyon wall to regain his balance. Looking once again at the approaching morning light, he sped off toward the cave trying to ignore the shooting pain it caused with every step he took. Reaching the entrance to the hollow cave, Jario listened for any sounds coming from the women. Not hearing anything and assuming they were sleeping, he bent down on all fours and crawled through the tunnel. Gritting his teeth, he grimaced each time he moved his shoulder. He could feel the wound reopen. Trying to avoid the branch embedded in his shoulder from raking against the tunnel wall, he limped along with his arm pulled close to his chest. Entering the cavern, he raised up on his knees and clenched his fists as he looked about the cavern for Lara.

"No," he howled, when he realized the cavern was empty. "I have failed. How could I have been so unwise? I left them too long, and they got away." He stood and slammed his fist against the cavern wall and howled until he could no longer stand the sound of his voice.

* * *

The news of the Eternity Ceremony for Lady Lara and Thomas spread throughout the castle and the surrounding area. Magna caught wind of the news and realized that Jario's plan must have had a disastrous end. She hadn't seen him since before her sister's kidnapping and wondered if he was lying at the bottom of the canyon, nothing more than a pile of ashes.

Magna sat alone in her chamber at Black Thistle Castle feeling sorry for herself but furious with the young vampire that had escaped her clutches. Her encounter with him had been disastrous. As a result of the fire he held in his hands, she had lost part of her arm and spent most of her time healing. It had slowly regrown, but it was weak and gave her frequent pain. Without the ability to take blood, it left her severely weakened causing her to sleep. Fortunately, the protection spell offered by Velsa had kept her safe and deterred anyone from entering her castle while she healed. She would seek revenge on the vampire when she was stronger.

Darkness had fallen as Magna woke to the warning sounds of someone trying to breech the protection spell. Reluctantly, leaving her chamber and entering the courtyard expecting to see someone from the Evergreen Army, she was surprised to see Jario standing on the drawbridge. Whispering the releasing spell, Jario passed through to the courtyard holding his arm close to his body as blood ran from his neck and shoulder.

"I failed," he angrily shouted. "I gave up my smoke and three favors to the old witch and have nothing to show for it."

Magna activated the protection spell and turned to Jario asking, "What did you expect? You should never have tried to kidnap her." With both hands on her hips, she glared at Jario. "Are you making Black Thistle Castle your new home?"

He looked over the ruins of the castle and knew that he was not welcome anywhere else. Half-heartedly, he nodded back at Magna. He would have to make do with this crumbling castle until he could restore it. He wanted an army of his own. He wanted an army that could destroy Evergreen Castle. Looking around the piles of blackened stones and then at Magna, he decided he would stay.

"You have a new master of the castle," Jario smirked, as he watched Magna's smile broaden. "I assume by your grin, you are happy I'm here."

Magna rubbed her hands together as she snarled, "Let's go plan our revenge."

Seeing a smile on Jario's face, she knew trouble would be prevalent in Evergreen's future and in theirs. Magna smiled wickedly as she envisioned the fun they would have as she took Jario's bloody arm. They vanished back to her dungeon leaving a wisp of swirling red smoke.

Chapter 26

The Great Hall was decorated with the traditional evergreen sprigs and wildflowers tied with blue cord. Torches lined the walls offering a flickering warm glow that caused shadows to dance about the stone walls. Wooden tables were dressed with candles set among the many bowls of wildflowers. The altar set beneath a large stained glass window proudly displaying the Evergreen Castle coat of arms. Against the cream linen draped across the altar, a blue cord rested next to a dagger and three crystal vessels, two filled with water and one that was empty. The food had been prepared and was waiting in the kitchen ready to be served. Everything was in order, and the festivities were ready to begin.

Members of the castle and invited guests from the Echo Bluff village began to line the wooden benches. A trio of musicians played softly in the corner of the hall filling the air with melodic sounds from strings and a wooden flute. Once everyone was seated, the Head of the Council, Omar, entered the hall wearing a long robe of dark green brocade. He was followed by Thomas dressed in blue breeches, a cream tunic trimmed in gold embroidery and polished black leather boots. Tate walked next to him dressed similar to Thomas but all in dark green. Thomas rested his hand lightly on Tate's arm as they made their way up to the altar. He was excited and wanted to see everything, but he held back his vision to wait until Lara entered the hall. He didn't want to miss any of their ceremony.

Tate leaned in close to Thomas and said, "Pull your vision, now. She is ready to enter the hall."

Thomas pulled on his vision with all his might, and he could clearly see Lara standing at the entrance of the hall. She wore a blue brocade gown embroidered with gold thread. Her shoulders were bare revealing the creaminess of her skin. Woven among the intricate braids of her hair were pearls strung on blue ribbons. She slowly walked toward Thomas, as Flora walked behind her carrying her long train. Reaching the altar, she turned and faced Thomas.

"My love, you look beautiful," he said, feeling his eyes start to water.

"And you, my love, are so handsome," she responded, with a smile.

Omar raised and lowered his hands asking for all to be quiet. He pulled a small leather book from his robe and opened it using the blue ribbon that marked the page.

He began to speak, "Today, we come to witness the joining of Lady Lara and Thomas for all eternity. Their love for one another is strong and true. It has been tested and proven to be worthy. Much has been endured and forfeited to prove their love. Thomas, do you pledge your trust, honor, love and protection to Lady Lara forever more?"

Thomas straightened his back and proudly said, "I will, forever more."

Looking at Lara, Omar continued to speak, "Lady Lara, do you pledge your trust, honor, love and protection to Thomas forever more?"

Lara smiled lovingly at Thomas as she replied, "I will, forever more."

Omar looked up at the crowd that surrounded the couple and asked, "Do you pledge your trust, honor, love and protection to Lady Lara and to Thomas?"

In unison the crowd responded, "We will, forever more!"

"As a symbol of their unity, they will begin the pouring," Omar announced, as he moved aside letting the couple advance.

Lara and Thomas made their way to the front of the altar and each picked up a crystal vessel filled with water.

"Each vessel is filled with water," Omar explained. "Pouring the water into the center vessel symbolizes the mingling of their souls. They will be forever changed as their souls will become one."

Lara and Thomas began to pour the clear water from their vessels. As the empty vessel received the clear liquid, the water swirled and changed from clear to a bright blue. Stepping back in front of Omar, Lara and Thomas waited as he took the dagger and cord from their resting place.

"By the offering of blood to one another, they unit themselves for all eternity."

Omar pierced their wrists with the point of the dagger. Pressing their wrists together, he wrapped the blue cord around their arms joining their wrists.

"It is with great honor, that I declare Lady Lara and Lord Thomas united for all eternity. Thomas, you may kiss your mate."

Thomas bent down and kissed Lara as the sound of cheering and clapping thundered about the hall.

Tate slapped Thomas on the back and said, "Congratulations!" Leaning toward Thomas, he asked, "May I kiss my new sister?"

Seeing Thomas nod, he stepped toward Lara and hugged her as he kissed her gently on the cheek. "Welcome to the family. I am proud to have you as my new sister."

"I am honored to have you as my new brother," Lara replied, and kissed Tate gently on his cheek.

The celebration was going strong, as laughter and music filled the hall. Through the side door, Baxter and Oliver entered carrying a large object draped with linen. Placing it on a wooden stand, they stepped away leaving it covered. Lara looked at Thomas wondering what the linen was covering.

Taking Thomas' hand, Lara asked, "What is it, Thomas?"

Leading her to stand in front of the object, he pulled the linen revealing a painting of Mona and the colt, Arrow.

"This is my wedding gift to you, my love," said Thomas.

He watched the surprise in her eyes and knew that he had pleased her.

"It is beautiful, Thomas," she said, as a tear fell upon her cheek. "I will cherish it always. We will place it above the hearth in our bed chamber."

Thomas let his vision fade. He wanted to save it for later in the evening. One by one, they were offered congratulations from everyone in attendance. It was a special time for all in the castle and a sign of good things to come with the uniting of Lara and Thomas.

After dining and dancing with Lara and too many other women to count, he took Lara's hand as he quietly asked, "Is it time to head to our chamber? I am tired of sharing you with everyone. I want you all to myself."

Lara smiled and responded by standing and pulling him to his feet. As they made their way to the door, everyone stopped to cheer and throw flower petals in the air. Laughing, they both hurried from the Great Hall and made their way to their bed chamber.

* * *

Thomas stood next to the bed anxiously waiting for Lara. He heard the bath chamber door open and the rustle of Flora's skirt as she passed by him toward the door. "Congratulations, My Lord," Flora said before leaving the room.

Hearing the door open and then close, he quickly pulled his vision. There in front of him stood Lara in a sheer blue gown tied at the shoulders with tiny blue ribbons. Her strawberry blonde hair was free of the ornaments worn for the ceremony and hung softly in loose curls down her back. The candle light reflected in her blue eyes, as her bare feet brought her toward him.

"You are so lovely," he said, as he kissed her mouth softly holding her face between his hands.

"Thank you, My Lord," she responded, with a smile.

Taking a step back, she looked into his eyes and pulled the ribbons from her shoulders, as he watched the shear fabric fall and puddle at her feet. He gasped as he took in the beauty of her body and felt his own shiver from the excitement. Running his hands over her shoulders, the sensation that they shared charged through his body as if electrifying every part of him.

He wrapped his arm around her waist and bent slightly placing his other arm under her legs. He lifted her up into his arms and placed her gently down upon their bed. His eyes scanned her body taking in every curve that belonged only to him. Pulling his linen tunic over his head and dropping it on the floor, he watched her eyes smile as she took in his naked body.

Silently, she leaned back against the feather pillows as she stretched out her arms to beckon him to her. "I have waited for you for my whole life, and you are finally here with me," she quietly whispered.

He entered the bed feeling her arms wrap around his shoulders. Her hands pressed against his back, and he felt the tips of her fingers begin to gently trace down his spine. Kissing her lips gently, he inhaled her lemon and mint fragrance that he loved so much. Feathering light kisses down her neck and over her shoulders, his hands gently caressed her back causing her breasts to press against his chest. His hands and mouth explored her body hearing her moan softly in approval. The touch of her hands against his skin made him tremble seeking more of her.

Feeling the heat growing within one another, Thomas moved his body over hers, resting his hips gently between her thighs.

"Lara, I love you," he said, as he prepared for the moment of bonding.

"I love you too, Thomas," Lara whispered, as she looked into his eyes feeling complete pleasure racing through her body.

As they joined their bodies and moved in rhythmic passion, Lara tilted her head exposing her throat. Thomas could sense her urgency building, as well as his own. He felt his fangs extend and the heat of his desire. Inhaling her scent, he was unable to wait any longer. He sank his fangs into Lara's throat, feeling her blood rush against the inside of his mouth. It tasted like wild honey. Lara arched her back feeling the electrifying pressure of his mouth and fangs upon her throat, as she grabbed the curls of his hair within her fingers. Without hesitation, she sank her fangs into Thomas' throat and reveled in the taste of him. The taste of sweet berry wine filled her mouth. Their release exploded as flashes of heat radiated through their bodies. They were bonded for all eternity.

Thomas rested with Lara's body nestled next to his. Her curves fit perfectly against his strong body, and he knew that he would never tire of the feel of it. Feathering kisses against the back of her neck, he could feel her body press closer to his own.

"Now that the bonding is complete, I can take my time to explore your beautiful body. I will never tire of kissing your sweet lips or the feel of them against my skin," he said, as he turned her body to face his. He kissed the tip of her nose and then her chin. "I plan on memorizing every inch of you."

Lara smiled and brushed the hair from Thomas' face. "You won't be the only one exploring," replied Lara, as her hand moved gently over his hard chest and then down past his stomach. "I have all of eternity to love you, and I look forward to a wonderful adventure with you, my love."

Feeling the heat begin to race through their bodies, Thomas pulled her close and put his mouth to Lara's ear. "It will be a wonderful adventure we can explore together." Thomas gently pushed her body back against the feather pillows and began to explore.

Epilogue

Running his hand over his shoulder made him think of his failed attempt at taking Evergreen Castle as his own. Jario stood with his back to Magna starring at the stone wall deep in thought.

I did not think everything through before I took Lara to the Canyon of Obscurity. I was too hasty. I should have brought her back to Black Thistle Castle. The protection spell would have offered me full control over her. Her army would have never been able to penetrate the boundaries. Next time, I will make sure my plan of revenge is perfectly thought out. There will be a next time.

"Are you still thinking about my sister?" Magna asked, as she twirled a strand of hair between her fingers. Stepping closer to Jario, she began to untie the laces of her corset. "What could you possibly want with her when you have me and all my talents?"

"She is my path to Evergreen Castle," shouted Jario trying to ignore Magna's enticing movements. "Once I have my revenge and Thomas has his final death, Lara and Evergreen Castle will be mine."

Hearing the protection spell alarm, Magna entered the courtyard to find Gusty and Buck standing at the drawbridge. With their hands on their hips, they looked confused to see Magna.

"More vampires," Magna said with glee, clapping her hands. "This could be fun."

"Let us pass, Magna," Buck yelled. "We did not expect to be blocked by you. Jario requested we come here to meet with him. He is expecting us."

Releasing the spell, Magna watched as Gusty and Buck made their way to the dungeon. Stepping into the dim chamber, they were greeted by Jario.

"I have asked you here to help me create an army for Black Thistle Castle," announced Jario. "We need to rebuild this castle and will need many to accomplish my plan for making it strong and powerful."

Buck rubbed his hands together after hearing about building an army. He had always wanted to lead an army. An army meant killing, and he reveled in the act of killing. Looking at Magna leaning against the wall, he noticed her playing with the laces of her corset.

Magna and an army would make his life very interesting, Buck thought, as he tried to pull his eyes away from Magna's body.

"When do we start rounding up the men?" Gusty asked. "I am ready to get started."

"Now," Jario replied, watching the grins appear on their faces. "Magna, leave us. We have much to discuss and don't need you to distract us."

Magna glared at Jario. Pursing her lips, she turned and stormed from the dungeon. They could hear her curses as she stomped up the stone steps and through the hallways. Finally, her screaming stopped, and the men stood in quiet.

After much discussion, Jario walked them back to the drawbridge and watched them speed away. As he slowly walked back across the courtyard, he stopped and turned in the direction of Evergreen Castle. Surrounded by the dark night sky, he staggered as he felt the depth of darkness and his hatred for Evergreen seize his soul. It seemed to energize his body, and his mind filled with the most evil desires for revenge.

I have become seized by obscurity, he thought, as he felt a strange surge of power race through his body.

Feeling the coolness of the breeze upon his face, he closed his eyes and envisioned his new army surrounding him at Black Thistle Castle. With a wicked smirk, he opened his deep red eyes as he raised his arm and pointed toward Evergreen Castle. "Get ready my sweet Lara. I am coming for you!" Jario shouted into the wind.

NOTE FROM THE AUTHOR

Thank you for reading Seized by Obscurity. I hope you enjoyed reading the story of Lara and Thomas as much as I enjoyed writing it. I would love to hear your reactions to their story. As a new author, your honest review would be greatly appreciated.

The journey for Lara and Thomas continues with Escaping Obscurity, Part II of the Evergreen Series, coming in the spring of 2015.

Website: www.authorjoannherley.com

Facebook: www.facebook.com/authorjhbooks

Email: info@authorjoannherley.com